Luna
CAGED

New York Times Bestseller

Margaret McHeyzer

ISBN-13: 978-0-6483670-2-4

Cover Design: Book Cover by Design
Editor: Debi Orton
Interior Formatting by Tami Norman, Integrity Formatting

www.facebook.com/authormargaretmcheyzer
email: hit_149@yahoo.com

Luna
CAGED

New York Times Bestseller

Margaret McHeyzer

Always fight for what you believe is right

PROLOGUE

DUCKING MY HEAD, I hope my hair hides my face.

"Luna, what are you doing?" the Elder asks.

"Gettin' in line," I explain. "I want to go where they go." I point to the line of boys in front of me.

The Elder laughs and shakes his head. He leans down to look at me. "Girls don't go where the boys go." He points to the line. "Girls don't need to be taught anything but how to cook, clean, and look after the men."

I stare up at him. I can feel my bottom lip quiver and my eyes well with tears. "But I want to learn too," I say in a small voice.

He places his big hands on my shoulders and turns me around. "Off you go. Get back to your chores," he says as he pushes me then gives me a light smack on the bottom. Not a hard one, just hard enough to hurry me along.

I do a small jump when he smacks me, and turn

to look at the line as it advances into the building. There's a word above the door, but I don't know what it says, of course. I can't read. Girls aren't allowed to read. It's one of the Elders' rules. Mommas and Sisters can't read, neither can any girl. But I want to learn, and the Elders always tell me I don't need to. I just need to learn how to clean properly, how to cook, and how to look after the men.

Turning, I notice Cain, shuffling along at the back of the line. He keeps looking at me, then back at the line. His brows are scrunched together as the line continues. "Elder Tom, why can't Luna learn with us?" he asks the Elder who hurried me away.

"Because we're men, and the men need to learn. But the girls aren't smart like us. They don't require it."

Cain lowers his head, and steps forward before lifting his face to look at Elder Tom. "Are they different than us?" he asks.

"Yes. They're girls. They don't have the same intelligence as us."

Cain lowers his head again.

"But why?" I ask, a little too loud. "Why aren't we as smart as you?" I quickly cup my hand to mouth, ashamed for asking.

"Luna." Elder Tom's face is angry when he notices I'm still here. He strides to me in deliberate, large steps. He grabs my shoulders, and shakes me as he pulls me forward to meet his angry stare. "Even if we *did* want to teach you, you're too dumb to learn. You proved it, because you obviously can't follow instructions. Girls are girls, and not as smart as men. Now get out of here!"

My shoulders droop. "Am I stupid?" I ask.

"All girls are," he responds in an even voice. "But we're men, and it's our job to look after you." A tear breaks free, and rolls down my cheek. "Go. I don't want to have to report this." He touches my nose slightly, smiles and turns. "Now class," he states to all the boys as he walks back toward the line, "let's go."

Cain looks toward me and sees me struggling to hold in my tears. He looks sad too. My shoulders slump and I turn to walk away. Why can't I learn? It's not fair.

I head back to the big house and find Sister Lorraine. She's on her hands and knees, scrubbing the floor. I'm still sad, but I can't really do anything about it. "Do you need help, Sister?" I ask as I automatically begin helping her without an answer.

"Thank you, Luna." She smiles at me, then quickly goes back to scrubbing the floor with the big brush.

My mind is going everywhere but here. I sit back on my heels and stare out to the common area, in front of the big house. "What's that?" I ask as I gape at the big round piece of wood sticking up in the middle of the dirt oval.

"You always ask too many questions, Luna. Best get back to work," Sister Lorraine says as she continues cleaning the floors.

"But no one ever tells me anything and I've always wondered what that is."

Sister stops for a moment, and carefully looks around. She leans in and whispers as quietly as possible, "It's a whipping post. But the Elders haven't had to use it for a while."

A whipping post? I don't know what that is. "What's a whipping post?" I ask with a tone matching hers.

"If we do something wrong, they tie us to it, and hit us."

I gasp as I flinch back. "I don't want to do anything wrong. Will they hit me?" More tears sting my eyes, but I do my best to hold them in.

"Not if you're a good girl. Come on now, we have to hurry up." She urges me with her eyes to keep scrubbing the floor.

When the floor is done, I help Sister up and we start toward the kitchen. I follow so I can help her.

"Luna!" I hear from behind me.

"Hi Cain," I reply as I turn to see him standing with a huge grin on his face.

"Let's go play," he says and bounces on the spot.

"I can't. I have to help Sister Lorraine."

"Cain asked you to go, Luna. He's a man, so you have to go," Sister says.

"Okay." I shrug my shoulders.

Cain is already running out the door, and I'm close behind him. He keeps running, until we reach the edge of the meadow. There's a huge wall there that's as tall as the sky. If I look up, I can't see where it ends. "Where are we going?" I ask. Cain stops, and he's puffing. He pulls out a little book from inside his pants and gives me the goofiest look on his face. "Is that a real book?" I ask, my eyes bulging with excitement. Cain's told me about them. I'm so excited.

"It is." Cain's smile is as big as what mine feels like.

He sits beneath one of the large trees, and starts flipping through the book. In my eagerness, I can barely sit still. "Can I touch it?" I ask as I hesitantly reach out to feel it.

"Here. I'm going to teach you how to read."

My mouth falls open, and I'm so happy I start to cry. I want to hug Cain, but the Elders would be angry if I did that. Boys and girls aren't allowed to touch unless the men are disciplining the girls, or unless we're serving the Elders. "Really?" I ask.

"Yeah, here." He flips the first page open, and there's a picture of an apple and a word.

"That's an apple," I say.

"Yep. Apple starts with A, the sound A makes is like this. *Ah… ah.*"

"*Ah*," I mimic him.

"That's so good, Luna. Now this here is a bus."

"A what?" I ask staring at the strange yellow picture on the page.

"A bus. The first letter is B and the sound it makes is like *ba*, like a sheep."

"Oh, *ba. Ba. Ba*," I practice.

"Yes!" he says and claps when I get the sound right.

"But what's a bus?" I ask.

He shrugs his shoulders. "The Elders didn't tell us. I asked once, and the men in the class started snickering. The Elders said we don't need to know right now."

"Oh." My gaze drifts away from the page, and I look toward the wall. "I want to know what a bus is, and what it does. Don't you?"

He shrugs again. "I don't know. Maybe."

Standing, I head straight to the wall. Leaning against it, I huff in frustration. "Why are they always telling us not to ask questions?"

"Luna." Cain stands and dusts off his dirty pants. "Stop it. You're going to get into so much trouble."

"But I want to know what's happening out there. I can hear noises. Sometimes at night, when it's quiet, I can hear things happening. All I want to do is go out there and see what's making the noises."

Cain's shaking his head. "You can't. There are only bad people out there. They'll kill you. Or hurt you. Please, Luna, don't ask any more questions. The Elders will get angry."

Something inside me shrinks, like it always does when I'm told to stop asking questions.

"What is going on here?" the voice is deep and booms from across the field. I look up to see Elder Steven coming toward us. His strides are large and angry. His face, even though he's not close, is red and furious. "What is going on?" he blasts again.

I don't like Elder Steven. He scares me the most out of all the Elders. "Noth-nothing," I stutter as I cower with my back against the wall.

"What's this?" He snatches the book out of Cain's hands, but his livid eyes are set on me. He flicks through the book. "What is this?" The rage in his voice now matches his face.

"We were just…" Cain starts saying, but Elder Steven silences him with a glare.

"I'm not asking you, son. I'm asking this witch," Elder Steven says in a gentler voice to Cain. He flips his anger back to me. "What are you doing?"

These tears are because I'm terrified of Elder Steven. "I'm sorry," I offer without even knowing what I'm sorry for.

Elder Steven steps forward, grabs me by the arm and starts marching me back to the main house. He's walking so fast, I have to run to keep up with him. Cain is closely following us.

"It's not her fault, Elder Steven. I wanted to show her what a book is," he tries to explain.

Elder Steven is furious. "It's alright, son. I know it's her fault."

I want to say something, but the hard hand on my arm tells me to remain quiet and not complain or cry. But I can't help the tears. They're falling on their own.

We get to the main house, and Elder Steven shoves me toward the whipping post. I fall to my knees, scraping them on the hard-packed earth.

"I'm sorry," I cry as I bury my face into my hands.

"Men and girls!" Elder Steven summons. Peeking out between my fingers, I notice everyone is gathering around us. What is happening? Why is he yelling for everyone? "Go and tell the other Elders we're about to have a whipping," Elder Steven says to some of the other men.

Crying, I try and stop my shaking. "I'm sorry," I keep saying.

Everything is happening in slow motion. Everybody is making their way out to the center.

"Get up," Elder Steven snaps at me.

Slowly, I stand to my feet but refuse to look up at anyone. I don't want to meet their eyes. *I'm so afraid.*

"What we have here is a girl who thinks she has the right to learn to read."

I hear a collective gasp. Looking up, I see the men standing to one side, and the girls are standing on the other.

"We have rules. And the rules are easy. Girls are to look after the men and the house. No girl has the intellect to understand what we do." The men snicker and nod their heads. The girls do the same thing. "Turn and face the post." Slowly, I turn. "Wrap your hands around it." I try, but I can't reach all the way around. "If you move, you'll get three more strikes."

My tears are falling fast now, and I'm sobbing in fear. I don't know what's going to happen.

"This is why the girls don't get an education."

The sound is what happens first. The slam of something on my back happens second. I scream in agony. It stings, and it's hurting. It feels like a hot rod is melting into my back. I barely catch my breath, when it happens again.

And again.

And again.

I'm just barely standing, and my back is burning in pain. "You will not try to trick another man into teaching you how to read, will you, Luna?" Elder Steven asks.

The stinging is so severe and I'm sobbing so hard, I can't catch my breath. I shake my head in reply.

"Girls are not able to learn. That's why we've created this God's Haven for you, so you're not taken advantage of out there where only death, poverty and disease is waiting for you. We are your family. Beyond the wall is death. Beyond the wall is evil. You will die if you leave. Only we can protect you," he says loudly.

Everyone is nodding.

"Next time you use your girlish charm to trick a man, I'll have you stoned to death."

"I'm sorry," I cry again. I'm still not sure what I did. All I know is I've been punished for it.

Elder Steven leaves me heaped on the ground in an absolute mess. Sister Holly comes over to me, and helps me up. "You brought this on yourself, Luna." She shakes her head as she helps me walk into one of the smaller houses. She takes me into a bedroom, lays me on my stomach and tends to my wounds. "You have to know, we're not like the Elders. We're not as smart as they are. Anyway, why do you want to learn? Learning is only for the men."

"Sister Holly?" I hear Cain's voice from the door.

Turning, I see him watching me.

"Yes, Cain?" Sister replies.

"I need to talk to Luna."

Sister Holly stands, gives him a nod, and leaves. He rushes over to where I'm lying, and gently reaches out to me. "I don't want to get in trouble again," I say pulling my hand back when he's nearly touching me.

He quickly retracts his hand, and lowers his eyes. "I'm sorry, Luna. I tried to tell them it was my fault, but they said as a man, it's never our fault. I'm sorry, really sorry." I watch as a tear falls by his feet.

"Please…" I say as I turn my head. "Just go."

I hear him back away. Then he says in a small voice, "I don't care what the Elders say. I'm going to teach you to read, because I know it's the right thing to do. I promise. But I'll figure out a way to do it so we never get caught again."

I blink the tears away and don't respond.

Why is it so bad to learn?

I don't understand.

CHAPTER ONE

"ARE YOU EXCITED?" Cain asks as we lay on the ground, looking up at the huge wall that encloses the Haven and keeps the world out.

"I don't know. What am I supposed to be excited for?"

"You'll be of age soon. That's a huge deal."

The sinking feeling in my stomach says it all. "Nope." I reach my hand out to meet his pinky. These are the only time we can touch, and even still we have to be careful not be caught by the Elders.

Since my first whipping when I was younger, I've been whipped twice more. Once because Cain and I were hugging, and the other time because I asked Elder William about the outside and he was sick of me asking about what happens beyond the wall.

"Maybe they'll marry us," Cain says bringing

me out of my thoughts.

"Not unless you've become an Elder." I let out a deep sigh, and reach further to hold his hand. "I don't want to be of age, and I don't want to get married to an Elder, and I don't want to have babies."

"But, that's your job. That's what girls are supposed to do." Even his disappointed tone doesn't like what he's saying.

"Cain, if you could leave, would you?" I ask trying to change the somber conversation of my impending marriage to an Elder.

"There's nothing outside for us, Luna. It's all sickness and death."

"I know that's what they keep telling us, but I want to see what's outside. Don't you?"

Cain huffs, and his fingers tighten around my hand. "I just want to be somewhere we can be together, without the Elders watching us, and beating you when we're caught."

"I don't think that's going to happen in here," I say in a small voice.

He sighs again. "I know." The sadness in his voice is enough for me to know how much he loves me. He's always loved me, like I've always loved him.

"I don't want to get married to an Elder," I say again. I look up the wall, and watch as a bird flies over. "I wish I had wings. Because if I did, I'd already be out of here. With you."

"There's nothing out there for us. Here we're safe and cared for."

"But how do you know what's out there? Unless you've seen it for yourself, you can't be sure."

"I've seen pictures in books," he tries to convince me.

"But the books are provided by the Elders. What if there *is* something? What if there's more out there than what they say?"

"I don't know," he replies hesitantly. "I know what you're saying, but what if it's *worse* than they tell us?"

"What if they're not telling us the truth?" I add. Letting go of his hand, I move to my side, and prop myself up on one arm so I can stare at Cain. He's so beautiful. He always has been. He's got the biggest brown eyes, and the sweetest smile. He has a dimple in his chin that never goes away, but when he smiles, it becomes deeper. "Don't tell me you don't think about that?"

Cain and I often find time to come out here and lay beside the wall. We think alike on most things, but I can tell how he struggles when I start talking about the outside world.

"I don't want you to marry an Elder any more than you want it. And I think you should be free to learn how to read and write, like we men are. But going outside? I'm not sure about that, Luna." He scrunches his face, and stares away from me.

"I wish I could marry you," he says in a smaller voice. "And I wish nothing more than for us to be together. But…" he trails off in a small voice. "As long as the outside world is filled with horror, disease, and death, then we're better off staying here."

Frustration begins to bubble. I want to scale the walls, and leave with Cain. If I'm wrong, then at least I will see it with my own eyes. "I want to see it for myself," I grumble.

"We have to trust the Elders. They haven't done anything to make us mistrust them."

"I want to see what a bus is. What it does."

"A bus? What on earth…"

"Remember? The book you showed me when we were younger. You showed me a picture of a bus, and you were helping me learn to read."

Cain sits up, crosses his legs, and smirks at me. "How do you remember that?"

I mimic his moves, our knees nearly touching. I can feel the warmth of his body rolling off him. I shift closer, our knees are now touching. My heart skips a beat. I love being close to him. He makes me happy. He always looks out for me, and when we're touching, he's the one who pulls back because he knows I'll get into trouble if the Elders catch us. "I want you to give me my first kiss," I say, choosing to put the memory of the bus behind me. "Do you think we can?"

Cain looks around, making sure no one can see

us, or is near us. He leans forward, and I automatically copy his body language. His face is so close to mine. I can feel his warm breath on my lips. I swallow the lump back, and try to calm my excited heartrate. He leans his forehead on mine. Closing my eyes, I take in this moment. Everything is right. We're so close. "I want to," he says in a husky voice.

"I want you to," I say, breathing in deeply and taking in his smell.

"But we can't. I wouldn't be able to live with myself if you got in trouble because we kissed."

Leaning back, I open my eyes. I'm disappointed, but also relieved. If an Elder saw us together, I would have received another whipping, for sure. They hurt. I have scars on my back from where Elder Steven has hit on the same spot. It's always with his belt… the buckle end. I think he enjoys whipping girls, especially me. I can hear the happiness in his voice when he's lecturing me and all the other girls. The Mommas and Sisters always tell me I'm to blame, because I don't follow the Elders' rules.

If whipping me is for my own good, I'm ready to see what's on the outside of these walls. It can't be much worse than life in here.

"I know," I say to Cain. "But I wish we lived in a time and place where we're free to touch, and to do what we want."

"We could run away," Cain says then adds in a

chuckle. "Although, I've never heard of anyone who's been outside the wall. I'm not sure where we could run away to."

"I wonder how many days it'll take to walk the whole way around the wall. Do you know?" I ask Cain, who's staring into my eyes.

"You're so beautiful, Luna." I blush and smile. "No, I have no idea how many days it would take to walk the wall. Elder Jacob said we'd get lost out in the wilderness." He points behind him.

I look to where he's pointing, and my mind starts to question everything. There's a huge part where we can't see the wall because the trees are so tall and dense. No one goes there, because the Elders say, beyond the trees is the wall, and they've been touched by disease. I don't know what that means. I don't know what a lot of things mean in Haven. I'd like to, but as the Elders often say, girls don't need to learn anything except how to cook, clean, sew and take care of the men.

Staring at where Cain's indicated, I really want to walk around the wall. Maybe I'll find something new. "One day, I'm going to walk the wall. I want to start behind the trees."

"What?" Cain leaps to his feet and paces back and forth. "You can't. You'll die."

"What if I don't die? What if I find something out there?"

"What do you expect to find? Disease? Death? No, Luna, I forbid you to go." He stops walking and crosses his arms in front of his chest.

"What do you mean, you *forbid* me?" I stand to face him, hands on my hips.

"You heard me. I'm the man, and you're the girl, you have to obey me."

"Over there, yes." I point to where the main house is. "But when we're here, just you and me, it's not like that." He lifts his chin in defiance. "You could always come with me." I step forward and place my hands on his folded arms. I don't care if an Elder sees me touching him, I'll take the whipping. "Please. Cain, I'm going crazy in here. I just need to see what it's like. I promise, if it's bad, we can come back."

"But the wall is diseased. That's what the Elders have told us. If you touch it, you could die. I can't…"

"Please. If… if…" I don't know what to say. I want him to come with me, but I don't know how to convince him. "If it gets too scary, we'll turn back."

Cain's resolve is not budging. "I can't let you do this, Luna. It's too dangerous."

"Cain, please?" I beg. I really want to go, and I know he'll protect me if we go together. "I need to see for myself."

"No, we can't. It's not safe."

"I can't live like this. I have to know." I'm so angry. Why won't he come?

Cain's shaking his head. His shoulders relax,

and he steps closer to me. Looking over his shoulders, he steps in and hugs me. "Luna," he whispers. I revel in this feeling. I can't believe how desperate I've been for him to embrace me, and how much I like it. "We can't."

He steps back, and looks over his shoulders again, making sure none of the Elders are running to drag me away and whip me. I notice the pained look on Cain's face. I think he wants to go, but at the same time, leaving God's Haven is terrifying to him. It takes me a long heartbeat to decide never to bring this subject up again. But it takes me only an instant to make the decision to go on my own. "Okay," I say as I look down at my feet, refusing to meet his gaze in case he can stare into my soul and see my plan.

"Promise me," he says.

I've never lied to Cain. I've never had to.

"I promise," I whisper, still looking down at my feet. The words come out of my mouth easily. And I hate myself for lying to him. But I need to get out of here and see what's on the other side.

And I have to do it soon. Because if I don't, I'm going to end up of age, and I'll have to wed one of the Elders, and knowing how much joy I bring to Elder Steven when he whips me, I'll probably be one of his wives. I see how horrible he is to them, and I don't want to be one of them.

CHAPTER TWO

"You'll be of age soon, Luna, and you'll be getting married," Sister Janice says as we prepare dinner.

"I know," I say, trying to pretend some enthusiasm. But inside, I feel like I'm dying. I don't want to marry any of the Elders. I don't want to get married at all.

"I overheard some of the Elders talking, and quite a few of them want you. That's got to be exciting. To be wanted by so many."

The thought of getting married makes my skin crawl. Most of the Elders are wrinkly, and some have no hair on their heads. Why do I have to get married to an Elder? Why do I have to get married at all? "That's nice," I say as I peel the heap of potatoes stacked on the counter.

"You should feel honored so many of the Elders want you. There was a girl, Theresa, none of the Elders wanted her. They ended up marrying her with Elder Edam, and you know what he did to her?" I shake my head. I don't recall anyone by the name of Theresa. "Elder Edam said he couldn't break her in, she wouldn't allow him to calm her. She was segregated from us, because of her temper." A shudder wiggles up my spine. "She couldn't give him heirs. It's said she was forced to the outside."

"Is that what it takes?" I mumble beneath my breath, knowing it's not loud enough for Sister Janice to hear.

"Hopefully you'll be with child the night you wed."

My stomach churns, and I fight hard not to vomit in front of Momma. I've heard some of the mommas talking about sex, and having sex with the Elders, but no one has actually told me anything about it. "I don't want to have sex with the Elders," I say. "Do I have to?"

"Hush, child," she snaps at me. "It's what we're supposed to do. You'll marry an Elder, and he'll be the one to look after you. But if another Elder wants you, then you'll go to him."

I cringe again. "What exactly is sex?" I keep peeling the potatoes.

Sister Janice's face reddens. "It's where the man puts his penis in your vagina."

"What? How?"

The tips of her ears grow pink. "You both get naked, you'll open your legs, and he'll tell you what to do. He'll push his penis in your vagina, and he'll get satisfaction from it. When he's done, he'll pull his penis out, and you'll be free to leave his bed if he's not the Elder you're wed to."

I'm completely disgusted. I can't even hug Cain without fear of being whipped, but the Elders get to put their penis inside me, and that's okay? How is that normal?

"Great," I mumble to myself. I want to ask a ton of questions, but I know if an Elder overhears, I'll be whipped for sure. They tell us often not to ask questions because we're too dumb to understand the answers.

But I don't think I'm dumb. I can't read or write, not past what Cain's taught me, but I don't think I'm stupid either.

"It's a great honor, child," Sister says again. "To be wanted by so many."

"How will they decide who gets me?"

"I don't know. We're not permitted to ask such silly questions. You'll know when they're ready to tell you, but it's usually before you're due to be wed." She leans in and whispers, "and that's when all the fun begins."

I scrunch my nose. Sounds revolting to me. All the Elders are so… yuck. And mean too. "How was Theresa banished to the outside world?"

"Why are you asking so many questions, Luna? You don't need to know the answers. We trust in the Elders. We believe in them, and have faith that all their decisions are to keep us safe. They are our masters."

Safe from what? They only ever tell us the outside world is dangerous, but I don't know anyone who's actually seen it. I want to see it, to experience it for myself. Why can't I? Every day I become more frustrated and irritated that I can't see.

"I know," I reply to her words. No use in asking anything else, because I'm not going to get an answer.

"Luna?" I turn and find Cain standing at the entrance to the kitchen. "Come." He gestures for me to go with him.

"I'm peeling potatoes, come help," I retort.

"Hush," Sister Janice nearly barks at me. "When a man calls you, you have to go. You know this, Luna."

I roll my eyes at Sister. "I know, but it wouldn't hurt for him to help. There's a lot of potatoes here." I eye the endless heap.

"The men don't do the cooking. What has gotten into you?" She clips me on the back of the head.

"He's got two hands, he can help," I grumble under my breath.

"Leave the potatoes and go."

I place the peeler in the sink, and wash my hands. "Bye." I lean in and give her a kiss on the cheek. The moment we're outside, I turn and follow Cain to the back where we like to lie beneath the wall.

But I quickly overtake him, and run ahead. "Slow down," he huffs from behind.

"No chance," I call over my shoulder and increase my speed.

We both run until we hit the wall, and I collapse to the ground, looking up to the clear sky. There's a fluffy white cloud hovering overhead. It looks lonely up there, all by itself.

Cain crumples in a heap beside me. His breath is ragged from trying to catch me. "You beat me!" he says in a high-pitched voice.

"I've been beating you for a while now."

"You have to let me win."

"No, I don't." I turn to face him. Our laughter quickly dwindles to silence. "Sister Janice said I'll have to have sex with the Elders." I cringe, still not exactly sure what having sex means. I got the basics. The Elder will put his penis inside my vagina, but what is the purpose of it?

"I know. They teach us what we have to do once we become an Elder."

"I don't understand, Cain. Why do I have to let them do that?"

"Because, that's what you're supposed to do."

I shake my head, and feel the frustration still growing. "But why?"

"It's what the Elders say girls are for."

"It makes me feel sick. I don't love the Elders like I love you. It's not right."

I hear Cain sigh. I don't turn to look at him. He's frustrated too, just not as much as me. I'm ready to leave my home, and search for more. But Cain's nowhere near ready to come with me.

"One day, we'll be able to be together. When I become an Elder," he says with confidence.

"Do you know when that'll be?" I ask with hope in my voice.

"Maybe soon?"

"When was the last time a man became an Elder?" I try to think back, but can't recall. Cain lifts his shoulders. "What do you think would happen if I said I don't want to marry?"

"What?" there's a definite tone of disbelief. "What do you mean? I've never heard of a girl refusing to marry. Like, ever!" He shakes his head, and twists his mouth.

"But, what if?" I ask again. "What if I said no."

"Then I think you'd get more whipping scars on your back," he says with a tinge of skepticism. But I can tell there's more to his voice. He shakes his head again, and draws his brows together. "Please, Luna," this time his tone sounds more like he's begging. "Don't find out. Every time they whip you, I hate watching it. It makes my stomach churn and I feel sick."

"I'll…" I want to say I won't, but reality is, I probably will. It doesn't make sense to me. Why do I have to follow these rules? What purpose can they have?

"Please," he begs again in a softer voice. "Please, don't fight them on this."

My heartbeat quickens as I gather the nerve to lie to Cain. I don't want to tell him an untruth, because I know what the consequences can be. But I don't want to marry someone I dislike, either. "Okay, I won't." The words come out way too easily. But Cain has to know this isn't right.

"Thank you," he whispers happily.

My mind doesn't quiet. It can't. I have so many questions, and no one will answer them. Cain doesn't want to see me hurt; I get that. But I can't do something that's not in my heart either.

"Luna." Elder Steven snaps his fingers at me.

"Yes, Elder Steven?" I ask as I approach him.

"More food." He points to his plate.

Tonight, I'm at the main house serving the Elders with Abigail and Sofia. Usually there are more girls to serve at meal times, but tonight for some reason they've requested only us.

"Yes, Elder Steven." I pick the platter up from beside him, and begin to add more food to his plate.

The Elders all have meals at the same time every day, and all the Elders are always here. Except for Elder William, who sometimes doesn't join them.

He's also one of the quietest elders. He doesn't say much. But I always notice how he sees and observes everything. He usually has a smirk on his face, and when I've asked him how he is, his reply is nearly the same every time. *"We're living in the safest place on earth, I'm very happy, Luna."*

I don't know what he means, but okay.

Once I've served Elder Steven more dinner, I go to stand back in my corner and lower my head. Usually their conversations aren't interesting. They talk about what's happening in here, so I tune out and ignore them — only responding when I hear my name.

"Luna," Elder Steven calls again. He hasn't called on Abigail or Sofia through this meal, only me.

"Yes." I step forward and wonder what else he wants. His plate is full of food, and his cup is filled with his special water.

"You'll be married soon, and broken in."

The other Elders laugh. One snorting and nodding his head.

"I know," I respond in a deadpan voice.

"There's a few of us bidding for you."

Bidding? "What do you mean?" I ask, my curiosity getting the better of me. I quickly clap my hand to my mouth, and wish I could take back my question.

The Elders all see the shock in my reaction, and some laugh harder.

"A few of us want to break you in," Elder Tom replies.

I can't help the shudder. I don't even know for sure what they mean, but the stirring of my stomach tells me whatever 'breaking in' means, it's not good. "How will you break me in?" Again, my stupid mouth has asked something I shouldn't.

"Luna!" Abigail barks toward me.

"I'm sorry," I reply, internally scolding myself.

"It means we're bidding on who is going to get you. You're like a prized filly." A prized what? What's a filly?

"At the moment, Elder Steven holds the top bid," Elder William says.

I blink at him, he barely ever speaks. But nothing is making sense. Top bid... breaking in. Ugh, they're so confusing. "If I knew what these things meant, I might be able to reply," I say.

"You're just a girl. And girls aren't smart enough to know," Elder Steven snickers. His eyes tell a different story though. He lewdly gawks at me, his gaze traveling the length of my body. Drinking me in.

Bile raises to the back of my throat.

"Whatever you want, I'll give it." He licks his lips while staring at me while addressing the other Elders.

I'm not sure what's happening. All I know is there's a sick, gross feeling tumbling around inside me. He's looking at me like I'm his prey. As if I'm the meal on his plate, and he's about to devour me.

"I think I might raise the stakes. Double what you're offering," Elder Tom replies.

Stakes? Offering? Ugh. Please someone explain to me what's happening.

"I like them young, and like them shivering with fear," Elder Steven replies. He's disgusting.

"What about me?" Abigail says in a small voice from behind us.

The moment I turn to look at her, she lowers her eyes to the ground. Her cheeks are pink, and I can see she's holding back the tears.

If she wants them talking about her like this, then I'll gladly stand back and let her take it. "What about you?" Elder Steven says, breaking the small glimmer of hope they'll turn their attention to her and leave me alone.

"I'm sorry," she murmurs without lifting her eyes.

I turn to look at the Elders. Elder Steven has a lifted brow, Elder Tom is scowling, Elder Morris's mouth is turned into a downward grimace, and Elder William looks amused. I want to yell at them. I want to tell them they're hurting Abigail's feelings and they shouldn't be treating her that way. It's not a nice thing to do. Can't they see how hurt she is?

"Stop it!" I say in a fleeting second of anger. I don't even clasp my hand to my mouth. This time I'm not ashamed of yelling at them. This isn't right. They're treating her so badly. I've never seen them be this cruel to anyone other than me. "Stop being so horrible to her. You all talk about respect, and how respect is earned. She's done nothing wrong, and you're being awful to her. You don't even have the decency to do it when she's not here." I'm so angry I'm shaking. My hands are trembling, but my voice is clear and precise. They have to know, what they're saying isn't right. It's making Abigail feel like she's nothing. If it's obvious to me, a mere girl, then it has to be obvious to them. They are the Elders.

Elder Steven sits back in his chair, and crosses his arms in front of his chest. Elder William chuckles.

Elder Morris stares at me, and a few of the other Elders relax in their chairs, with eyebrows high, and with disgusted looks on their faces.

"You think you have the right to talk out of turn, Luna?" Elder Samuel asks.

I was waiting for Elder Steven to scold me, then to stand and drag me out to the whipping post, where I was sure to get at least several lashings for being aggressive with them.

I turn to look at Abigail, her chin is lowered and tears are rolling down her cheeks and falling to the ground. Sophie too is standing against the wall, not saying a word.

The air in the Elder's dining room is thick. My own heart thrums so fast I can hear it as it beats rapidly against my chest. I feel sick. But I need to let them know how wrong it is to speak about Abigail like she's nothing. I know we're just girls, and I know we're not smart. But I also know, the way they're treating her, is wrong.

"I'm not out of line," I finally pluck up the courage to reply. Though my voice is tiny, and filled with fear. "You were being mean," I say in a tiny whisper. The room is silent, my voice although small, carries far. I'm waiting for everyone to come running in, ready to punish me.

"Quadruple the amount," Elder Steven says in a serious tone after a long, drawn-out silence.

"Are you kidding?" Elder Morris asks.

"No one has ever gone for that much," Elder William responds. "Ever, in all the time we've been here."

What are they talking about? My curiosity wants to ask, but I know I'm pushing a fine line between getting punished, and remaining unscathed.

Elder Steven is smirking. He's drinking me in, ready to consume me. He makes my stomach churn. I really don't like him, and right now, I'm not happy with any of the Elders. They've all been horrible.

"Unless there's a better offer, looks like you've got yourself a prize," Elder William says, then laughs.

What's a prize?

I don't get a chance to ask before Abigail bursts into tears and runs out of the room. The Elders cast a bored eye in her direction, before turning and resuming their food. Pigs. All of them.

"Luna, get me a drink," Elder Morris says and holds up his cup.

I want to tell him to get it himself. He's got two legs, and two arms. I stare at him and feel my lip turning up in revulsion. Poor Abigail has just run out of here, and none of them are seeing if she's okay.

I quickly pour Elder Morris's drink, then run out to find Abigail. They can whip me if they want. I really don't care. Abigail is sweet, and she's always quiet and never gets whipped. Unlike me, I'm always in trouble. Though I'm learning to control what I say and do. Especially around the Elders.

"Luna!" I hear Elder Steven call for me as I run out the room. I'm not going back until I know Abigail is okay.

"Sister," I say as I come to a stop in front of Sister Rachel. Momma Edith always has a stern look on her face. She and Momma Kim, Elder Steven's wives, aren't very nice. All the Sisters are scared of them, and whenever they pass them, they lower their eyes. Momma Edith and Momma Kim usually tell us all what to do. One time, Sister Polly was told to clean the bathrooms and she didn't because she ran out of time. For many days afterward Momma Edith and Momma Kim made Sister Polly clean each bathroom from dawn until dusk with her own toothbrush. Then they made Sister Polly cook for all the younger ones, too. Sister Polly was exhausted, finally breaking and apologizing for not being able to get to her chores. Momma Edith and Momma Kim, both gave her a nod, refusing to speak to her. They're tough, and can be just as nasty as the Elders. Truthfully, Momma Edith scares me just as much as Elder Steven.

"What are you doing?" she asks with a stern look on her face. Her eyebrows are drawn in together, and her mouth is turned down as if she's appalled by my presence.

"Um, Abigail," I stop speaking and lower my eyes. "She's upset."

"Aren't you serving the Elders?" she asks, her tone becoming more harsh. I don't have the courage to speak. I simply nod and look down at my shoes. "Then I suggest you get back in there and do the job you're supposed to."

"But Abigail is upset. She ran out crying."

"And Abigail will be dealt with for leaving without permission."

"But…" I try again. Momma Edith simply

points and waits for me to go back into the Elders' dining room. I know she's not going anywhere until I'm back in there serving the Elders. Dragging my feet, I head toward the dining room.

The moment I hear Momma Edith's steps leaving, I sneak around the corner and wait until she's completely gone. I poke my head out quickly to make sure she's not coming back. Then I wait a little bit more.

Oh, my goodness. My heart is beating so fast and loud. I can feel my blood pumping through my body. I sneak another look, just to make sure. Then I run out to go find Abigail. But I have to stay close to the walls, so Momma Edith doesn't see me. If she does, I'll be in so much trouble.

I sneak around trying to locate Abigail. I go in and out of the houses, slinking in, searching, then leaving as quickly and quietly as I can. But I'm careful, making sure I stay out of sight.

I get to the last house, and when I'm inside, I can hear someone crying. I know it's Abigail. I have to find her and make sure she's okay. "Abigail?" I whisper. But her crying is loud enough to drown out my calling to her. "Abigail!" I call again.

The crying stops just as I head into one of the bedrooms. Abigail is sitting on the bed, and she's wiping the tears away from her face. "Luna," she says in a small, angry voice as she holds in a sob. "What are you doing here?" she snaps toward me.

"I've come to check if you're alright." I head over to her, and sit beside her on the bed.

She moves away from me. "Really?" She tilts her head slightly to the side. "Or did you come to rub in how much they want you and how they don't want me?"

"What?" I question. "What do you mean?"

"It's always been you." She stands from the bed, and starts pacing inside the room. There's not much space between the beds lining the walls, stacked three high.

"What do you mean?" I ask, perplexed, again.

"It's always been you, Luna. Since the first time you've been whipped, you've been the favorite."

"I was the favorite because I was whipped?" That doesn't even make sense.

"It's always, Luna this and Luna that. They look at you like they worship you. And I look at them with the same look. I want them to want me the way they want you."

I scrunch my nose. "You can have it. You can have them all if that's what you want. I never asked for this."

"Don't you see? The more you do things wrong, the more they all want you. If I did something, like I spoke up in the dining room, I'm totally disregarded, like I'm nothing."

"Abigail." I stand and try to go to her.

"Don't!" she half shouts at me and steps away.

"Don't touch me. If it wasn't for you, then they'd want me."

"You can have them!" I say again. They repulse me, I don't want any of them touching me or looking at me the way they do. Why can't she see that? "Honestly, Abigail. Whatever I can do so they look at you and not me, I'll do it. Just tell me what that is."

"Please!" she spits toward me and rolls her eyes. "You love how they look at you."

"No! I don't. If they would leave me alone, I'd love that."

"You're such a liar, Luna. You parade around in front of them, swinging your hips, and flicking your hair. Just because you're the prettiest one here, it doesn't mean you have to rub it in our faces. We know! You get it? WE KNOW!"

I stumble back, hurt by her accusation about how she thinks I see myself. "Abigail." I shake my head as I try to find the words I need. "I think you're beautiful. You have the most beautiful hair, long, blonde, and so shiny. You are perfect."

"Yeah, right." She rolls her eyes at me. "I don't believe you." She lifts her chin in defiance and walks past me, hitting me with her shoulder on the way out. "Don't ever talk to me again, Luna. It's all your fault they like you better than me."

I stay glued to my spot, shocked by Abigail's admission of how she feels about me. Worse still, how she sees me.

I feel so bad. Is it my fault the Elders like me better than her? I don't want them to, I'd be glad if they never looked at me again.

I take several deep breaths, holding in the tears that want to escape. Does everyone else think the same way?

Does Cain?

Slowly, I move out of the room and head back to the Elders dining room. Hopefully no one's noticed how long I've actually been gone for.

As I leave the bedroom I see Elder Steven leaning against the wall beyond the doorway. "Luna," he says and crosses his arms in front of his chest.

"Elder Steven," I respond and lower my head.

"Are you okay?" I nod my head but refuse to make eye contact. "Get back to your chores." I nod again and hurry past him.

I don't turn to look at him, but I can feel his shrewd eyes on me, watching as I scurry away.

Without lifting my head, I rush to the dining room to find the Elders still there, laughing and eating. The only person missing is Elder Steven. I slink back in, and Elder William quickly catches my gaze. He smiles, and nods his head, as if he knows what's happened. It's only a few heartbeats later when Elder Steven returns, takes his seat and resumes conversation.

It's just a wide-eyed Sofia and myself.

There's a dark, looming tension quickly

tightening in the room. I can feel it. The threat of danger hanging, ready to pounce.

I'm not sure why the air is so tight. It feels like something is about to happen. Something bad... very, very bad.

CHAPTER THREE

THE SUN HAS risen, fallen, and risen, and something is definitely off. Momma Edith ignores me. Momma Kim has been asking me questions about Abigail and what happened in the dining room, and where I disappeared to.

"Luna, you're in the dining room," Momma Kim instructs.

"Yes, Momma Kim," I reply and move to the dining room to serve the Elders their meal.

When I get in there, Abigail is already waiting. When she turns her head to see me enter, she scowls, rolls her eyes, and then looks away.

"Hello, Abigail," I say trying to make peace with her. But my efforts are futile. She doesn't even acknowledge me. This hurts my heart, because I really don't think I've done anything wrong.

"Abigail," Elder William says and snaps his fingers. "Drinks." He points toward everyone's empty cups.

Abigail smiles, takes a step forward and picks up the jug with water to fill their cups. She quickly returns, stands beside me and Elder Tom calls, "Abigail, get us some more bread."

She lifts a brow and smiles at me. As if she's saying, *'Ha ha, they want me more than you.'*

I, of course, couldn't care less, and I'm pleased she's happy.

"Abigail, more food," Elder Steven says, not even giving her a chance to stand still.

"Abigail, take my plate and bring me another."

"Abigail, bring me something to wipe my face."

"Abigail, we need more to drink."

All the Elders are calling on her, and not me. I'm not sure if they're doing this to teach me a lesson, or to teach Abigail the lesson. And truth be told, I don't care either. I know I'm only a girl, and I should be grateful my destiny is being fulfilled with the Elders wanting me, but I don't care. I really don't. I'd rather explore what's beyond the wall and see the sickness and death for my own eyes. Yes, I know, I shouldn't want to, but there's got to be something more. We can't be the only ones who are healthy, who die only we're supposed to. Surely, there has to be more.

"Abigail…" The Elders keep calling on her, and she's reveling in the glory. If I could, I'd leave her to serve on them, and I'm positive she'd love it. All their attention is on her.

Standing back, I watch as she floats from Elder to Elder. She's the happiest I've seen her in a long time.

When dinner is finished, I'm standing exactly where I was when I entered. I haven't been called on to serve the Elders. All the Elders are chatting between themselves, paying me no due and giving Abagail all the attention.

"Luna, you can leave," Elder William instructs with a dismissive wave of his hand.

I quietly leave the dining room, and go to find Momma Kim to ask if she needs me to do anything else. I hope not, because I really want to go down toward the wall where Cain and I spend time together and we can talk freely without the Elders listening to what we say.

Walking toward the main house's kitchen, I can hear Momma Edith and Momma Kim talking in low hushed tones. I shouldn't listen, but something in their pitch tells me to try and hear what they're saying. They can't see me, and I can only see their backs, but I know, just by the way they have their hair pulled back, it's Momma Edith and Momma Kim.

"They're planning something for her," Momma Edith says then laughs. "From what William said, she's not going to react the way she did in the dining room again."

Oh no! It's because I left to go after Abigail, they're going to do something to me. I feel sick. What could it be? Am I going to be whipped again?

My heart sinks into my stomach, and I think I'm going to throw up.

"Did they say what?" Momma Kim asks with eager enthusiasm.

"He just said, she's got a big lesson to learn."

A small tortured sound escapes past my lips, and I instantly clap both my hands to my mouth. I step back, making sure they can't see me, and run as fast as I can away from here. I'm out of the house, and around the back before either Momma Edith or Momma Kim see me.

I keep running until I'm at the wall, and when I get there, I burst into tears. Leaning my hands on my knees, and bent at the waist, my tears keep falling. Why do they hate me so much? Am I really so different? So different they want to keep punishing me?

"Luna!" Cain's voice usually calms me, but not now. I'm too worried about the whipping they're going to give me.

"Go away," I cry, and don't bother looking up to him.

"What's happening?"

I try to calm my breath, and control my tears, but knowing what's coming makes my whole body hurt.

"Luna," he calls again. This time the urgency in his voice makes me stand, and throw myself in his arms. I know we're not allowed to touch, and I know I'll get whipped if the Elders see us, but I don't care. They're going to punish me anyway, so what does it matter if they add more strikes of the belt for hugging Cain? "You can't do this," Cain whispers, but hugs me tighter against his body.

"Please, please don't let go," I plead and continue crying. "I'm going to the whipping post anyway, I don't care if they see us touching."

"What? Why?" he asks, his voice filled with worry.

I can't bring myself to break away from him. His chest is to my chest, and I can feel the heavy beat of my heart echoing against his. I like this closeness; this bond is warming although I know it's not allowed. "I did something, and I heard Momma Edith and Momma Kim talking, and they said the Elders are going to punish me."

"What did you do?"

I don't want to break our connection, but I have to. Dropping my arms from around Cain's waist, I back away from him and lower my gaze. He's going to get mad at me, not because I did what I did, but because he doesn't want to see me getting whipped again.

"It started when Abigail, Sofia and me were in the dining room serving the Elders." I walk to the wall, and sit with my back against it.

"What happened?" He mimics my position against the wall. I tell Cain what happened, and he's sitting next to me with his mouth gaping open. "Luna…" he draws out my name, as if he's in pain. "Why would you do that? You should've just shut your mouth and not said anything. And why did you go after Abigail? That was a real dumb thing to do."

Suddenly, something inside me snaps. I stand and begin to pace in front of Cain, trying to calm the anger bubbling deep inside the core of my body. "No," I say, still trying to find my thoughts. "The way they were talking to her, it wasn't right, Cain."

"We don't question the Elders. They only say and do things for our own good."

"How can it be for our own good, when Abigail was in tears? How can you say that what they did was for her own good? How? They were talking to her like she was nothing."

"Well, she is just a girl," he says innocently.

"Is that all I am? Just a girl?"

"Come on, Luna." He stands and dusts off his pants. "Now you're really being dumb."

I stare at him in shock. I *cannot* believe he said those words. To me, of all people. "Something is not right, Cain. It's not right here. Why should we get treated like we're nothing? It doesn't make sense. The girls do all the work. We cook, and clean, and make sure you all eat before we do, yet we're treated so badly. I get whipped because I ask questions. Why does that happen? If you were to ask anything, they'd probably tell you how proud they are of you, but because I'm a girl, it's like I'm not allowed to think for myself."

"Luna, if you haven't figured it out, it's because girls aren't capable of learning. You can't do anything more than cook, clean and make sure we eat — as you said."

"But we're not even given the chance. What if I'm smarter than you?" Cain laughs, a laugh so loud, it angers me even more. "And why do we have to wear these long dresses, and we're not allowed to wear pants? You're allowed to wear shorts when it's hot, and we have to wear these ugly long dresses all the time. You don't have to wash the dishes after you've eaten, but we have to wait until the Elders eat, then the men eat, then we're allowed to eat. Why? Why should it be like that? Why can't we all eat together?"

"Whoa, back up, Luna. Not being allowed to wear pants, is obvious. Because that would mean you're like us, and you're not like us, you're different. You're not as smart as us, and you can't do the things we can do." He's sounding like an Elder, and I hate it.

"Like what?" I challenge with a hand to my hip.

"You can't do what we do," he says again.

"Tell me something specific you do that I can't."

"You can't read," he replies with a clipped tone.

"I can't read because I'm not allowed to learn. What else?" I push, getting angrier with every heartbeat. Cain leans against the wall like he's thoroughly amused by my anger. "That's right, there *is* nothing else."

"You're just being a girl." He rolls his eyes and smirks.

I want to slap him across the face, but I won't. Even though I'm so angry, I have to use all my control to hold back. "I can do everything you can, Cain, and let me tell you, I can do more."

He rolls his eyes at me again. "I don't know why you're angry at me, you're the girl who's speaking out of turn in the dining room." He crosses his arms in front of his chest and tilts his head to the side.

"I'm angry at you, because you're not listening. I'm trying to say there's got to be more. They always tell us how we need to respect them, but they weren't giving Abigail the same respect they demand. Doesn't it work both ways? If they want respect, shouldn't they show it too?"

"They don't have to show respect, Luna. They're the Elders. They can do whatever they want."

And here is the obvious problem.

This is so frustrating to me. Can't he understand what I'm trying to say? "But then, if you see the Elders treating us girls badly, does that mean it's okay for you to do it too?"

"I would never," he responds immediately. "I couldn't be mean to you."

"Really?" I turn to walk away. "You just said

I'm only a girl and I can't do what you can, so you actually were nasty to me."

I walk away, not waiting for him to respond. I'm angry, and right now, I can't deal with Cain and what he thinks. I need to get away from him, before I start to believe he's like the Elders. I love Cain way too much, and for that reason alone, I need to put some distance between us.

"Luna!" he calls.

"I can't do this, Cain. Not now," I say without turning around.

I walk the base of the wall, and try to think about everything.

The thing I know for sure is that the Elders will whip me. There's no doubt in my mind. They're angry at me for speaking out in the dining room. I know this because of how they were treating Abigail when we were serving. They were making it obvious they were angry at me, because I felt bad for Abigail.

The only questions are, when will they whip me, and how long will the lashing last?

I hope my back won't be soaked in blood when they finish with me.

It doesn't matter. I'm going to get out of here, so they can never whip me again. I'll take *this* whipping; I have to. But I will never let them do this again, because I'm going to find a way to get past the wall.

CHAPTER FOUR

"LUNA!" I AWAKE with a startle. Momma Edith's stern voice is calling me.

Opening my eyes, I see it's still dark outside. But when Momma Edith calls… you wake, and you don't ask questions. "Yes, Momma?" I reply groggily still trying to open my eyes and wake.

"You're in the dining room," she says from the door way not lowering her voice.

I look around the room to all the girls who are in here with me, to see if any of them have stirred. "Okay," I say and turn to look at Angel. She stirs beside me, but doesn't wake.

"Now," Momma Edith barks.

I'm surprised none of the other girls have woken with her loud and severe tone.

"Yes, Momma," I say again. This time I don't look around me, I push the covers off my body and sit up in bed. Momma Edith disappears from the doorway, and I place my feet on the cold floor. A shudder rips through my body as my pumping blood chills. It's so cold. The sun hasn't come up yet.

I head out and find Momma Edith and Momma Kim both standing out near the kitchen. They're both staring at me. Momma Edith looks amused, and Momma Kim has an eyebrow raised. "You're in the dining room."

Drowsily, I nod my head. "Okay," I reply as I begin to walk toward the dining room.

"First, take these with you," Momma Edith calls.

I head back to where they're still standing, and Momma Edith points toward the kitchen. I walk in to the aroma of freshly baked bread. Yum, I love bread when it's just pulled out of the oven. There's a distinct smell to fresh-baked bread; it's like the sun warmth hitting freshly churned butter.

I want to sneak a piece, but I know the Elders must eat first, and once their appetite has been curbed, then it's the men, then once the men are finished, then it's the girls' turn. I hate being a girl sometimes. The fact I have to wait to eat last doesn't make sense to me. Why can't we all sit and eat together? But I don't dare ask. I'd probably get whipped if I did.

My mind instantly goes to my impending punishment. They haven't called me out to the whipping post yet, and I'm becoming more anxious the longer I wait. I don't understand though. Usually, the whipping happens immediately, but they're delaying this for some reason. It gives me more opportunity to prepare myself. At least when it happens, I'll be ready and not panicking so much. But I do wish they'd get it over and done with.

"Straight to the dining room," Momma Kim says.

"Yes, Momma," I reply as I pick up two of the bread baskets and head out of the kitchen. Momma Edith is standing back, watching me carrying the bread.

I'm salivating, drooling over the fresh, crusty bread. I want to sneak a slice, but I know that'll mean extra strokes with Elder Steven's belt.

I head down the hallway leading out toward the open area where the whipping post is. I hear noises coming from a bedroom. I don't know who was sleeping in there last night, so I'm not sure who's making the noises.

The sounds are muffled, but I know it's a man because the tone is heavier and deeper. It's kind of like a grunt, crossed between a pant, like when you're running really, really fast, and the breath is drained from your lungs. It sounds like that. But the panting and grunting sounds like it's coming from various different voices, which makes me think there are a few men in there. I wonder what they're doing.

I listen closely in case someone needs help, but then I shrug my shoulders and keep walking.

I have no idea what's going on. It doesn't sound like anyone needs help. Maybe some of the men went for a run, and now are out of breath. I don't know. It's not really my business. They're the men, they're allowed to go running. But why would they run before the sun has come up?

I decide to keep going to the dining room and set up for the Elders to arrive for their breakfast. I really have no idea why Momma Edith woke me when it's still black outside. Maybe after they eat, they're going to whip me. Maybe she wants me to do all my chores first so the other girls don't have to do my chores as well as theirs.

Heading into the dining room, I see it wasn't cleaned from the Elders' dinner last night. I quickly begin to clean, because the Elders will be mad if they come in here and find it in such a disgusting state.

I finish cleaning the dining room, then I get clean plates, cups, and cutlery out. Placing them on the table, I set the table the way we're taught. The cups to the side, and the cutlery on the other. From when we start serving the Elders, we're shown how they like it, and that's how we set their table at meal times.

I start shuttling between the kitchen and the dining room, bringing the food into the dining area. Josie, Mary, Sara, and Halle are all in the kitchen, preparing the food. "Hello," I say when I enter the kitchen and see them cooking.

"Hello!" Halle says as she turns to look behind me. "Are you on your own?" she asks.

Usually there are more girls to serve, but it hasn't crossed my mind until now that I'm on my own. I've been so busy cleaning that I didn't even realize it. "I'm not sure who's supposed to be helping, but it's only me." I shrug my shoulders and wonder who's missing. Hopefully it's Abigail, because I know how much she enjoys the attention the Elders showered her with last night when we served them.

"Momma Edith told us to make extra today."

"Why?" I ask.

Halle looks at me and tilts her head. "Like she's going to explain it to me." She huffs and looks behind her. My gaze goes to where she's looking, and I let out an annoyed breath. Great, I have to take all these things to the dining room on my own. My annoyance is growing, and I think Halle can tell. "I'll help you," she whispers. "But I can't stay in there."

"It's okay." I offer her a smile. "I'll do it, I don't want Momma Kim or worse, Momma Edith to catch you helping me. You might get whipped."

Halle clasps her hand to her mouth in horror. "Surely I can help a little." But I can tell by her voice, she doesn't want to get in trouble.

"I'll do it." Although it would be nice to get help. Squaring my shoulders, I quickly begin the process of moving all the platters of food to the dining room. When I'm done, I stand back, proud that I managed to do this all myself.

The Elders all begin to arrive. Elder William is the first in, and he doesn't even meet my gaze. He ignores me, like I'm not even here.

Elder Steven then arrives, his face is red and there's beads of sweat on his forehead. Then Elder Tom and Elder Morris enter, both with the same flushed cheeks and glassy eyes as Elder Steven.

None of them make eye contact with me. They're laughing, as if they're sharing a personal joke.

"Luna, drink." Elder Steven snaps his fingers toward me.

I pick up the jug, and pour his drink, then make my way around the table. The Elders are talking among themselves, and I look around to see if another girl has come in to help me.

"What are you looking for?" Elder William asks.

"I was wondering if anyone else will be coming in to help me."

The Elders laugh, and Elder Samuel shakes his head. "No, you're on your own," Elder Samuel replies.

I'm on my own. Great. I have to do the entire service by myself. "Who would you have if you could, Luna?" Elder Steven asks.

Without thinking, I blurt, "Abigail." Why did I

say her name? Because I know how much she enjoys dining service. And that means the Elders would be enamored with her and leave me alone.

"Abigail?" Elder William asks.

"She enjoys the attention." I clap my hand to my mouth. Why did I say that? It's bad enough I said Abigail's name, now I'm telling them why I want her here.

"Abigail won't be in the dining room for a while," Elder Steven laughs.

"Why?" I ask.

Elder Morris chuckles too before he adds, "Abigail is slightly broken."

"Broken? How? Is she okay? What do you mean by broken?" I rapidly respond, concerned by their words. I'm not sure what they mean, being broken is something that happened when Brett broke his arm, and when Simon broke his leg. Has she broken her arm? Or her leg? But their laughter and menacing gleam to their eyes, tells me something bad has happened.

"She won't be on service for a while," Elder Steven replies and adds another laugh.

"How can you be laughing when Abigail is hurt? Does she need help?" I ask, a fire in my belly taking over. I hate how non-caring they are.

Elder Steven eyes me up and down and sits back in his seat. "You're a real prize, Luna. I look forward to the night we wed." Involuntarily, I shudder from the sick tone to his voice. I'm not sure why, but my skin covers in goosebumps, and bile quickly rises to the back of my throat.

"A prize?" I question. "What do you mean?"

"Luna, bread." Elder Tom snaps his fingers at me.

Picking up the bread basket, I head over to him, still waiting on an explanation. But it doesn't appear Elder Steven is going to give me one. I place a piece of bread on Elder Tom's plate, and turn to look at Elder Steven, who's not even paying any attention to me. Instead, he's laughing with Elder William who's sitting beside him as they share a low-voiced conversation.

I really, really hate being a girl. Especially when they don't answer a simple question.

My stomach flips with annoyance. I can feel the heat rising throughout my body heading to my face. I bite on my tongue so I don't say something that's sure to earn me more whips when they give me my punishment.

"She'll learn," I hear Elder William say, low, beneath his breath.

Who'll learn? I want to know more. I shouldn't be listening, but I want to know who they're talking about.

"Next time she speaks out of line, she'll remember what happened," Elder Morris replies. Quickly, his gaze flicks to me, then back to Elder Steven. He lifts a brow, and smirks then lifts his stare back to me.

Everyone stops talking, and turns to look at me. Elder Steven's face is showing the most amusement. All the other Elders stare at me as if I'm intruding. "Do you have something you want to say, Luna?" Elder Steven asks.

I purse my lips together, choosing to be quiet because I know what the consequences will entail. "No," I reply in a low, yet annoyed voice.

"Really? You look like there's something happening in that pretty, *young* head of yours." He sits back, crosses his arms in front of his chest, and grins at me again.

I hate the way he's talking to me. It's like he's making fun of me but thinks I'm not smart enough to understand.

"You said I was a prize. What do you mean by that? And how are you not worried about Abigail? If she's broken, then she probably needs help. I just…" I stop talking, knowing what I've said is already too much.

"You're what?" Elder Steven asks, encouraging me to finish what I started. But I feel like they're waiting for me to say what's on my mind, only to whip me more.

"It doesn't matter." I bite down on my tongue and wince in pain. Quickly, I feel the metallic taste of blood in my mouth from biting down too hard.

"Please, amuse us all." Elder Steven gestures toward all the Elders who are sitting at the table. "You're what?" he asks again.

I shake my head, still refusing to talk.

"I do believe it's time for a whipping," Elder Tom says and laughs while rubbing his hands together.

I crinkle my brow at him, and this makes Elder Tom laugh even more. "You get pleasure out of whipping me. But, I ask you what you mean by saying I'm a prize, and you won't reply. I can't see how this is fair."

"Fair? Who ever said anything about fair. You're merely a girl. A thing. An object. Don't ever forget that, Luna," Elder William answers.

What? An object?

"But you told me Abigail is broken, then you're laughing at those words. If it was Cain, or another man who was broken, you'd be worried. Why are you laughing about Abigail?"

"Because Abigail needed to learn a lesson," Elder Morris answers. "Besides, Cain and the other men wouldn't be broken the way Abigail is."

"A lesson? I don't understand."

"And that's because you're a girl. Girls aren't smart. As you've clearly shown all of us," Elder William responds and everyone laughs.

But I don't find any of this funny. "This is wrong. You're not answering anything I'm asking, you're just sitting there, laughing." I gesture toward them. "Why can't you answer me?" I feel my pulse elevating, and my anger reaching a new level it's never been before. Even when I've been whipped, I've never been this angry.

"You're a prize because of your spirit," Elder Steven finally answers.

"My spirit? What's that?"

"You've always been different from the other girls, and you've always been *more* than the other girls."

"Isn't that the truth?" Elder Samuel mumbles with a sigh.

"You won't break, and for that reason, you're a prize," Elder Steven says.

I don't know what they're talking about. I can't understand.

I stiffen my shoulders and turn back to wait for further instructions from the Elders. They continue talking, but I barely hear anything they're saying. Elder Steven answered my question. I just don't understand what he means.

Maybe he's right, maybe they're all right. Maybe, I'm not like the others, even for a girl.

CHAPTER FIVE

ONCE THE ELDERS finished eating, I clean the dining room and get it ready for their next meal. Doing it on my own is hard. I wish Abigail, or Sofia or Halle, or anyone, would come help. But I'm the only girl on dining room duty. Which means it's all left for me to do.

By the time I'd finally finished and went to take the last dirty dishes to the kitchen, the sun was high in the sky. The Elders would be gathering again soon for their next meal. But I still had to wash their dishes. Thankfully, I'm not on cooking duty too. I wouldn't have been able to manage it if I was.

"Luna, can you help when you've finished?" Bethany asks as I enter the kitchen to the main house.

"What do you need?"

"The men have eaten, and then it's our turn. Can you help with the meals?"

I sigh. I haven't eaten yet, but I know neither have any of the girls either. Except for Momma Edith and Momma Kim; they eat with the men.

I want to grumble and sigh and tell her I worked the Elders dining room without help, but I know Bethany must be hungry too. "Are you by yourself?" I ask as I look around.

"No, Christine and Rose are with me. Momma Kim told Rose to do something else, and Christine had to go to the bathroom. But we're so busy, I'm not sure we're going to have time to eat because I need to start on the Elders' lunch."

"Why can't the men help?" I mutter beneath my breath.

Bethany giggles and her cheeks flush. "You're so funny." *I wasn't trying to be funny.*

I head over and stand beside her. "What do you need me to do?" I ask looking around the mess of the kitchen.

"Can you cut the lettuce, and then the tomatoes." She pointedly looks to the side, and I see a stack of both lettuces and tomatoes. "I'm sorry, I know there's a lot. But I have to make some more bread, and de-feather the chickens." She looks behind her, and in a box, there are many dead chickens, laying ready to be plucked. "And I'm not sure if I'll even have time to eat," she says and then slumps her shoulders and lets out a tiny sigh.

I can't let her do all of this on her own. "We'll

get through it. Hopefully Christine is back soon and we'll finish what needs to be done." I start cutting the lettuces, and before long Christine is back.

Her cheeks are flushed and she appears like something's wrong. "Are you okay?" Bethany asks my silent question.

Christine nods her head. She's a wife of Elder Morris. He married her when she came of age. The Elders keep telling us when we come of age, we're mature and ripe. I'm not sure what that means. "Elder Morris wanted me to…" she stops talking and shakes her head.

"To what?" I ask before thinking.

"Nothing," she replies and lowers her chin to her chest. Out of nowhere, a small cry leaves her mouth. "He told Elder William he could have me whenever he wants. Elder Morris sat and watched while Elder William…"

I scrunch my mouth, not sure what she's going to say, but whatever it is, I don't think I'm going to like it. "He's what?" I ask.

"So crinkly. He's not very nice." I'm not sure what she's talking about. "He told me to lie down while he placed his penis in my vagina. Elder Morris had his penis out and he was stroking it. I didn't like it."

"Why didn't you say something?" I ask.

"Luna!" Bethany and Christine scold me together. "We're girls. We have to do what they want us to. It's our duty."

"If you don't want it, then you should say something," I say with passion. The fire in my tummy is growing.

"What?" Christine claps her hand to her mouth. "We aren't allowed to say anything. It's not our role as an Elder's wife to say anything. It's our duty to obey." She shakes her head and looks as if she's angry at me, or disgusted that I said anything.

"It doesn't seem right to me," I say as I look down to the lettuce and continue chopping.

"Get used to it, because once you marry an Elder, if another Elder wants you, you have to do what they want," Christine says.

"What's it like?" Bethany finally asks something instead of just listening.

"What's what like?" Christine responds.

"When he puts his penis in your vagina. Does it hurt?"

"The first time it did. But not now."

"Do you enjoy it?" Bethany asks shyly.

"Ewww. No, but I know the Elders do. Elder Morris always has a flushed face, and sweats, and once he's finished he tells me how good it feels. I just lay there until it's over. Sometimes he wants me to sit on him, but mostly, he tells me to lay down and open my legs."

"Flushed face and sweating?" I ask,

remembering back to when the Elders began arriving for their meal. A lot of them had flushed faces. *Yuck.*

"Always for Elder Morris. But Elder William, he's…" She scrunches her nose and shakes her head. "I shouldn't speak ill of any of our Elders. They protect us and take care of us. We must serve them and look after them as a thank you for protecting us from what's out there." She points to the window, indicating the wall.

"But what *is* out there?" I ask.

"Death and sickness. You know this, Luna," Bethany replies in a serious tone, and downturned brows.

"I only know what the Elders tell us. I'd like to see it for myself."

Both gasp. And I lift my gaze to see them both staring at me. "No one has ever been beyond the wall," Christine murmurs in shock.

"There's nothing but death and sickness," Bethany says again. "Why would you want to leave when everything you need or want is right here in God's Haven. We have perfection."

"Because that's what the Elders have been telling us since we were young. What if there's more out there?"

"More?" Bethany clutches at her chest. "There is. Haven't you been listening? Death and sickness. There's something wrong with you." She looks back to the bread she's kneading and shakes her head with disgust. "The Elders tell us how lucky we are that they protect us. We should be grateful."

"I am. I'm so grateful, that's why it's my duty as a girl, to cook, clean, and look after the Elders," Christine says with confidence and a smile.

She's gone from not liking Elder William putting his penis in her vagina, to being grateful. It's no use saying anything more about what's beyond the wall, because they don't want to know what's out there.

"Luna!" I turn to see Abigail.

"What happened?" Bethany draws in a sharp breath.

I stand still, shocked by what I'm seeing.

Abigail is barely standing at the door. She's bending at the waist, gripping onto the door frame. Her lower half is covered in blood. "Are you broken?" I ask as I rush over to her.

She snaps her head up at me. Abigail has tears streaming down her cheeks. Her lip is split, and she has black shadowing beneath her eyes. "It's because of you!" she screams at me.

"Me? What happened? I didn't break you." I remember when Brett had a broken arm, and he didn't have anywhere near as much blood as Abigail has now. I quickly check her arms, and neither have blood coming from them.

"You did this to me, Luna. You!" she screams again, then doubles over, crying in pain.

I'm so helpless, I have no idea why she's saying I hurt her. I haven't touched her. "What did I do?" I try to help, but she stays folded into a ball, crying. "Abigail, I'm sorry. So sorry," I say. I extend my hand and attempt to touch her, but I'm so frightened. If she's broken, maybe she needs the Elders to help her. Like Brett needed the Elders' help. "I'll get the Elders." I straighten and turn to run outside.

"No!" she screams. "Don't get them."

"What's going on in here?" Momma Edith's voice booms.

We look up at her, not really sure what to say. Everyone is quiet, and the only sound is Abigail's pained cries. "She's broken, Momma," I finally say. "She's broken." I point to her lower part where the blood is dark and soaking into the dull material of her long dress.

Momma Edith's mouth turns up into a small smile. "Broken she is," she says as she eyes Abigail. "This happened because of you, Luna." Her steely gaze turns to find me.

"How did I hurt her?" I ask. Not understanding.

"They said there's only one Luna," Abigail whimpers. "It's because of you."

I step back, my look going between Abigail's misery, and the satisfied gleam in Momma Edith's eyes. "I don't understand," I say in a small voice. "Who said that? And why…" My voice trails as my brain attempts to make sense of what's happening and what I'm seeing.

"The Elders. They all said I had to be taught a lesson, because there's only one Luna, and I'm never to speak out of turn again. But you." Abigail straightens, although I can see it's painful and difficult for her, and points to me. The hatred in her eyes is enough for me to know she doesn't want to be my sister ever again. "But you, you can do anything you want, because you're the girl they all want." She clenches her jaw together, and makes her hands into fists. "I hate you," she spits.

"But I…" I shake my head as I take several small steps backward.

"Don't you ever talk to me again."

Momma Edith steps in front of Abigail, cutting my view off of her. "Well, well, well, seems like that mouth of yours has gotten one of your sisters in trouble. Maybe you should think, before you challenge an Elder again. Maybe you should just shut your mouth, and keep quiet." Momma Edith raises an eyebrow at me.

"I didn't mean to hurt you," I whisper. But I'm horrified at myself. I know this happened to Abigail because of what I said in the dining room when we were serving the Elders. I shouldn't have said anything. I shouldn't have tried to help Abigail. It's all my fault. "I'm sorry," I cry, turn, and run out of the kitchen.

CHAPTER SIX

IT'S TURNED DARK, and I've been sitting out here by myself. I'm glad Cain didn't come to find me. I'm glad none of the girls, the Sisters, the Mommas, or the Elders came to find me. I can only imagine what everyone thinks of me.

It's because of me Abigail is broken. Somehow, I did that to her. *I* made her bleed.

The moon is in the sky, with only a few stars twinkling near it. There's a chill in the night air, raising goosebumps on my skin.

My long dress doesn't keep me warm. I really should go back to the houses. If I keep away from the main house, maybe I can slip in without the Elders or the Mommas noticing.

The crazy thing is, I don't want to go back. I want to stay out here, without any of them.

I lie back, placing my hands beneath my head, using them like a pillow. I can feel the dirt beneath my fingers, and don't even care that I'll be dirty. Staring up at the inky sky, I can't help but wonder about my life. I don't fit in. I want to see what's beyond the wall, see the sickness and death for myself.

The Elders are always telling us how hopeless it is beyond the wall, how we're special because God chose us to continue the human race. Whenever I ask why we're special, I'm always met with silence.

How can I not wonder about what's beyond the wall when they don't answer any of my questions? I don't understand.

My heart cries when I think about what they have done to Abigail. They broke her, and told her it's all my fault. If she wasn't trying to be like me, they wouldn't have hurt her. It bothers me to know *I'm* the cause of her pain.

This only makes me more determined to get out from behind the wall. Maybe I'm not worthy enough to stay here. I'm not sure I can control my tongue. If I see the Elders treating other girls like they treated Abigail, I don't know if I can stop myself from saying something about it.

Not to mention, I'll be married soon. Likely it'll be Elder Steven. I don't like him. I know I have to respect him, because it's a rule we must abide by, but I don't. I don't think he deserves my respect just because they tell us to do it.

"Luna," Cain's voice quietly echoes in the

distance.

I wish I could melt into the ground so Cain can't see me. Not because I don't like him, I really do, but because I want to be left by myself.

"Luna," he calls again.

I sit myself up so Cain can see me. The moment he does, he walks toward me, and sits down.

"I couldn't see you. It's dark," he says.

"I know." I lay down again, looking up at the sky. "Why are you out here?"

"Because it's past curfew, and no one has seen you since the sun was out."

"I didn't want to be seen," I respond while staring at the moon overhead.

"Is it because of what happened to Abigail?"

I sigh as my heart breaks more. "It's because I don't belong here. And yes, because of what happened to Abigail. It's my fault she's broken."

"We had to gather by the whipping pole, and they told us not to speak to you."

"I thought something like that would happen."

"And they told us when we see Abigail we have to spit on her."

A regret sinks in the pit of my stomach. "Because of me," I whisper and wipe at a tear leaking from my eye. "If I didn't say anything, Abigail wouldn't have been treated like this."

"Yes, it is *all* your fault," Cain replies in a stern voice.

"I'm so sorry." I bring my hands to my face and cry into them. "I didn't want anything to happen to Abigail. It's just, they were treating her so badly. It's not right."

"They can do whatever they want; they're the Elders. And when the day arrives that I become an Elder, I'm going to do whatever I want."

"Will you talk to girls the way they did?" I ask through my tears. "Because if you do, I don't think we can be friends any more."

"When I become an Elder, I'm going to change the rules."

This makes my tears stop. It's not often Cain speaks out about the rules the Elders have. "How?" I ask.

"Girls will be able to learn if they want. And we'll all sit together to eat meals."

"Really?" I ask with so much hope in my voice.

"Yes, really. And we can marry anyone we want. Girls won't have to marry an Elder if they don't want to."

"Oh, that sounds like a place I want to live," I sigh. "Wouldn't it be wonderful if you'd become an Elder before I need to marry an Elder."

I can see Cain shaking his head. "Becoming an Elder is something only a select few men are chosen for, Luna. And we have to prove ourselves as worthy, and be trained to become one. The Elders choose very carefully in order to teach their ways."

The crisp quiet drowns out any thoughts in my head. I stare up at the moon, trying to let the peace take over. "I feel bad, Cain. For what happened. I can take the silence from everyone, but I'm not sure Abigail will be able to take everyone spitting at her."

"She's going to have to."

"How was she? I mean, how was she after the Elders ordered everyone to spit on her?" I shake my head in disbelief. My entire body hurts because of what I've brought on Abigail.

"She went to the bathroom, and hasn't come out since."

"The Elders believe this is best. For her and for you."

I turn to stare at Cain. "Do you really think spitting on someone is best? Because I don't."

"It's what the Elders think."

Anger is once again beginning to bubble. "But what do *you* think?" I ask.

"It's what the Elders believe," he says again.

"Yes, I understand it's what they believe, but do you? Do you honestly think not talking to me, and spitting on Abigail is the right thing to do?"

Cain turns. His eyes narrow, and his jaw tightens. "I don't understand what you're asking, Luna."

"I know you're saying the Elders believe in this punishment, but do *you* believe in it too?" I can't say it any more simply. "I mean, did you spit on Abigail when you saw her today?"

He takes a few breaths before he responds. "I pretended to, but I didn't."

"Why did you pretend? Why didn't you walk past her and actually spit without pretending?"

"Because Elder Morris was beside me."

I shake my head, slightly disappointed in Cain. "Cain…" I say his name slowly.

"Yes, Luna."

"That hurts me. The fact you still pretended to do it, when you know you shouldn't."

"I had to," he argues.

"Why?"

"Because Elder Morris was next to me. I told you already."

"It hurts me, because what if the Elders told you to whip me, would you do it?"

"But it wasn't you, it was just Abigail."

"Don't say it's 'just' Abigail. That makes her seem like she doesn't bleed red. We all bleed the same color. Whether we're a girl, a man or an Elder. We all bleed the same."

"But I had to," he tries to say again. Does he really believe what he's saying?

"Cain, can you leave? I'm really upset, and I don't want to be around you right now. Seeing as you're so good at pretending, can you go back, and if any of the Elders ask, tell them you couldn't find me. I'm going to sleep out here."

"Luna, I can't do that. I can't not tell the truth."

"But you already did. You pretended to spit on Abigail. That's not telling the truth." Cain grumbles and I turn away from him. "Please, Cain. Leave."

I can hear the rustling of his pants as he stands. But I can sense he hasn't left. I can also hear his breathing. "I'm sorry, Luna. I'll try to be more like you." And then he leaves.

I don't want anyone to be more like me. I want everyone to be their own person. I want everyone to think for themselves, and realize spitting on, and not talking to people, isn't right. It might be to them, but it isn't to me.

I close my eyes, and try for sleep.

If everyone is told to ignore me and not talk to me, then it doesn't really matter if I go back now, or when the sun rises. Hopefully, they won't even notice.

It's peaceful here, and before I even have a chance to turn on my back to stare at the sky, a deep sleep takes me to a world I can only dream about.

The ground beneath me rumbles and I startle awake.

Opening my eyes, I notice the moon and the stars are still in the sky. It's darker, much darker now. Stretching, I jolt up with the ground still vibrating beneath me. Panic quickly rises as I have no idea what's happening. The houses are far away, and if I run real fast I should be able to get there quickly.

But voices stop me from leaping to my feet and running toward the houses. The voices are deep, though hushed. My eyes take a few heartbeats to adjust to the dark, and I try to focus on where the voices are coming from.

Once I'm awake, I try to make myself small, so I can't be seen or heard. Quietly, I crawl along the edge of the wall toward the husky, low voices. As I get closer, I instantly recognize them as Elder William, Elder Steven, and Elder Samuel.

"We need some medication. Make sure you get Tylenol," Elder Steven says.

"And yeast for the bread. Edith also needs her magazines," Elder William says, then chuckles. "God forbid I forget the fucking magazines." All the Elders laugh together.

God? Fucking? Magazines? What are all these things they speak of?

"What are we going to do with the girl? She's been holed up in the bathroom the entire day. We had our fun with her, but now, she's used goods," Elder Samuel says.

What does, 'had our fun with her' mean? I crawl closer, to try to see what they're doing.

Elder William has something white in his mouth. He takes it between his fingers, and moves it from his mouth and lowers it, then brings it to his mouth again. Smoke escapes every time he repeats those motions.

"I don't want her now," Elder Steven laughs. "Lousy lay."

"See if one of the others want her," Elder William responds as he waves his hand dismissively.

"She's going to be a problem," Elder Samuel replies.

"Then get rid of her. Like the others."

Get rid of her?

The others?

Who are they talking about?

"And Luna?" Elder Samuel asks.

"That little spitfire is all mine," Elder Steven says. "She's gonna be wild. Just like a bronco." He starts making a thrusting movement with his hips. Elder Samuel and Elder William laugh.

"As long as we get our turn once you're done with her."

"I don't know about that. I don't think I'll ever get my fill of her. That mouth… I can't wait to use that mouth of hers. She's going to look so good on her knees." He rubs his hand over his crotch and I instantly feel like vomiting. But I keep it together and listen. I know I shouldn't, but I have to.

"Keep it in your pants, Casanova," Elder William teases Elder Steven, and the three laugh. "Back to business."

"How long do you think you'll be?" Elder Steven asks.

"I shouldn't be longer than a few hours. I've got to get the medication, and Edith's magazines, and Kim said to get her candy."

"Pick me up some M&Ms," Elder Steven says.

"Do you want anything?" Elder William turns and asks Elder Samuel.

"A five-foot hot Asian. And a bottle of bourbon."

I have no idea what they're asking for. And considering I've never heard them speak like this before, I can only assume, I'm not *supposed* to hear any of this. I'm keeping this to myself. I'm not even going to tell Cain.

"See you on the other side." Elder William walks a few steps, and gets into something. It's like a box. Actually, it looks like a smaller version of the bus I remember from the book Cain showed me when he tried to teach me how to read. That bus was big and yellow, but this is small and black.

The small black thing isn't very loud, but as it moves, it shakes the ground. Not a lot, but enough for me to fall to the grass, and try to hold on. But my curiosity wants to see where it goes. And how it gets beyond the wall.

The black thing goes through a hole in the wall, then the hole is filled by the wall again. I've walked this wall ever since I was able to, and have never seen any way out. Is there really a door in the wall? A way to leave?

Is it really that easy?

I wait until Elder Steven and Elder Samuel are far enough away, before I begin to crawl even further from them. I'm so curious. I want to know more. But I know if they catch me out here, I'm going to be in a lot of trouble. I might be whipped so badly I wouldn't be able to sleep on my back again.

Although my mind is buzzing, I need to get back to the house, and hopefully, not get caught coming in after dark.

CHAPTER SEVEN

"You're on dining duty," I hear Momma Edith's voice say.

I open my eyes and look around. Waking in bed, I'm instantly taken back to the previous evening, when I lay in the grass beside the wall and overheard a conversation I'm not entirely sure actually happened.

"Yes, Momma," I say, jumping out of bed, and going about my morning routine.

I'm itching to get to the wall to see if there's any sign that what I think happened, did happen. I know I have to wait until my morning duties are over, but so many questions are swirling around in my head.

"You'd best hurry," Momma Edith says with a tight smile and suspicious eyes.

"I will." I swiftly get ready to serve the Elders. I rush into the dining room, and find Abigail already standing at attention. "Abigail," I say, surprised by her presence. My gaze automatically drifts down to her lower half. I'm not sure what to expect. I saw her blood-soaked dress is now clean, and free of any blood stains. "Are you okay?" I wait for her to answer, but she stares past me, completely ignoring me.

Oh, that's right. The Elders gave instructions to ignore me. And she's following their directions. I should be like her, follow the rules, do what they say. I should at least *try*. But, my brain doesn't seem to work like that. The more they say I can't, the more I want to try. The more they say girls are dumb, the more I want to know so I won't be stupid. The more they say, the more I want to defy. Not because I'm bad, but because my head wants to know *why*.

"I hope you're okay," I whisper as I stand beside her.

Out of the corner of my eye, I notice how her hard exterior softens. Only a touch. Her lips that were pursed into a tight, thin line, relax. And I see her eyes drop to the floor. But that only lasts until the Elders begin to arrive. They each enter the dining room, and completely disregard Abigail.

Elder Steven speaks first, "Luna, don't you look refreshed and radiant."

"She certainly does. Did you sleep well?" Elder Morris asks.

I can't believe the Elders. They would've been

told about Abigail's breaking, and the blood that covered her dress, and they're talking to me instead of her? Especially when they told everyone else not to talk to me?

I can't help myself. I sneak a look sideways to Abigail. Her eyes are red, and a few tears have escaped. My heart saddens to see how they're ignoring her and how hurt she is by it.

I shake my head, genuinely upset by the way the Elders are treating me and Abigail.

"Elder Morris asked you a question," Elder William bellows in his big, angry voice.

Ordinarily, I'd shake with fear, but all I'm feeling right now, is pity for Abigail, and disgust with the way the Elders are treating us so completely opposite.

"Fine," I reply with a short, clipped tone.

"My spitfire is back," Elder Steven says while rubbing his hands together.

I close my eyes, just to regroup, then open them and turn to look at Abigail.

Although she's crying, she's hardened her features, and lifted her shoulders. She's not happy with me for speaking the way I am. I pull myself back from what I want to say. I want to scream at them, and tell them they're being mean to Abigail, but images of her blood-drenched clothes flash before me. She said the blood was because of me. I can't do that to her again.

"I slept well, thank you," I say as I square my

shoulders, pick up the jug and fill the Elders' cups with liquid.

"You're looking particularly beautiful," Elder Steven says again.

His voice makes the hair on my arms stand. He makes me cringe. But I have to push on, *for Abigail*. "Thank you." The words sting as they leave my mouth. The false smile I've plastered on my face, feels even worse.

"You, get us bread," Elder Steven addresses Abigail. Tears still cling to her cheeks. This saddens me even more.

Abigail moves forward, and I notice how she's walking. *Slow.* Is she still broken? I can't imagine she's healed, not after all the blood I saw. I want to go to her, take the bread basket out of her hands and serve the Elders myself. Not to get her in trouble, but to give her a chance to heal properly. I debate with myself, should I, or shouldn't I? Would she be punished if I do? *Probably.* I can't do that to her. It's not right.

Although my heart is hurting for Abigail, I stand in my spot and watch her.

"Get me a drink," Elder Samuel commands. He doesn't direct it to either of us, so I grab the pitcher and begin to walk over to him. "Not you, Luna." He smiles at me, showing me too many teeth. "Her." He points to Abigail.

Abigail is placing bread on everyone's plate, and she still has more to go.

"I can do it," I say, and immediately regret speaking.

Abigail gasps, and pauses. My head is telling me to pour the water, my heart is saying, 'Abigail was broken because of you.'

The blood. *All the blood.*

"I'm sorry," I whisper, go and place the pitcher back where I found it, and stand in the same spot I was before I moved.

Abigail is still staring at me.

Something passes between us. I want to hug her and tell her I'm sorry. The worried look on her face screams at me; *I can't go through that again.* I can see the worry, and the fear. I don't even know what happened to her, all I know is the hate in her voice when she yelled at me, *and the blood.*

Abigail bites on her bottom lip, worrying it between her teeth. She turns away from me, continues placing the bread on the plates. She slowly makes her way over to the pitcher, picks it up, and pours the water into the cups.

The Elders are laughing at something. I have no idea what. I've turned off listening to them. My heart is hurting too much to care what they have to say or what they're laughing at.

"Get me another plate," Elder Tom demands. The tone in his voice tells me, the request isn't for me. His voice is harsh. Like a hot knife slashing through freshly churned butter.

A tear falls from my eye. I quickly wipe it away.

Rocks fill my stomach with dread. I hate this. Knowing if I help, Abigail will get in trouble. If I don't help, Abigail will be treated like she's nothing more than the mud on the Elders' shoes they scrape on rocks before entering their homes. Either way, Abigail will be punished.

"Luna, come here." Elder Steven gestures with his finger.

I swallow the lump in my throat, and walk toward him. "Yes, Elder Steven," my voice cracks.

"Are you okay, my sweet girl? You look so sad. Do you need anything?"

I can't believe him. He's horrible. No matter how I respond, it'll make Abigail feel worse. If I say yes, then Abigail will be broken again. If I say no, Abigail's heart will shatter because they're paying attention to me, and not her.

I lower my eyes, and shake my head. Choosing to not say a word.

"She's my sweet girl," Elder Steven says.

A shudder rips through me the moment he calls me his 'sweet girl.' I want to react, but I hold back on everything I want to say.

The breakfast service passes, and the Elders all shuffle out of the room, leaving Abigail and me to clean and set up for the next service.

The room is filled with a chill, not because it's cool, but because Abigail has ice in her heart. I would too. "I'm sorry," I whisper to Abigail as I try my hardest to do more work than her.

"Don't talk to me," she says in a slow voice through clenched teeth.

"Please," I beg.

"You're dead to me." She drops the plates on the floor. They smash into so many pieces. I rush over to her, drop to my knees and begin to clean them up. "It should've been you they did *that* to, not me."

My head jolts up, and I stare at her retreating back. "Who did what?" I call. She turns and glares at me over her shoulder. The look in her eyes is deadly, like she wants to hurt me. But she doesn't answer. She shakes her head, and looks forward as I'm left in the Elders' dining room to clean.

Dropping my head into my hands, I cry.

It feels like the sun is moving, and most the day has drifted by, but I push myself up off the floor and continue cleaning. The broken plates take me the longest, and I'm careful not to cut myself as I pick up all the shattered pieces. With tears still clinging to my cheeks, and my heart broken, I finish setting the dining room, ready for the next service of the Elders.

"Luna, have you eaten?" Momma Kim asks.

"No, Momma," I answer. I'm not sure my stomach can handle any food.

"Feed the young, then if there's anything left, you can sit and eat. You're on dining room for lunch."

"But I just came from there," I say and instantly

regret the words.

Momma Kim isn't as mean as Momma Edith, but she's close to it. She stands in front of me, folds her arms in front of her chest, and tightens her jaw. "Excuse me?" she asks. But I know it's a question I shouldn't answer. Dropping my tear-filled eyes to the ground, I shake my head. I'm not speaking. It's safer to say nothing, and do as they instruct. Safer for everyone around me. "Feed the young." This time, her voice is hard.

"Yes, Momma." I turn to leave to round up the young.

CHAPTER EIGHT

THE SUN FALLS, and the moon rises. And finally, I'm left to myself. The entire day has been the same. I've been on dining duty with Abigail, and the Elders have been horrible to her. *Nasty and mean.*

I've wanted to say something all day. Whenever my voice wanted to be loud, and to tell them to stop, I'd bite on the tip of my tongue or the inside of my cheek. But all I've done is cry.

Abigail has been a mess. And no wonder. I would be too.

No one has spoken to me, with the exception of the Elders and Momma Edith and Momma Kim. Even Cain walked past me, looked at me, lowered his head and kept going.

I don't blame him. I don't want him to be whipped, or broken because of something I did. But it made me feel terrible.

I'm out near the wall, lying on the ground,

looking up at the moonless, starless night. More tears fall. But the rumble in my tummy and the hurt in my heart ease the tears. I haven't eaten since sunrise, and my tummy really hurts. Momma Edith had me cleaning the bathrooms in Elder Steven's house. He stood at the door, watching me, and making groaning sounds when I moved forward to get into the hard-to-reach spots. I really don't like him. There's a door in Elder Steven's house that's always locked, and we can't get in to clean. I tried to go in, and he told me, *'That's a room you'll discover once you're my bride.'* Just the sound of his voice makes my stomach churn, but when he adds a smirk and his eyes travel the length of my body, it makes me feel really sick.

The deep sound of the bell is heard, even as far as out here. It tells us all, it's time to get inside and we're not allowed out. Sometimes they call curfew, and that curfew is at sundown, way before the bell is rung.

But I don't want to go inside, even though I know they'll be looking for me. I have to, I suppose.

Standing, I smooth my dress down, making sure there's no evidence of the dirt or grass from where I've been lying. I walk, as slowly as I can toward the houses. I wonder where I'll sleep tonight. Will it be with my sisters, or will I be forced to sleep outside under the darkness of the night?

Honestly, I hope it's outside. At least there, it'll be quiet and I won't have the stares of eyes looking at me and not saying anything.

As I come inside the house, I walk from bedroom to bedroom trying to find a bed where I can lay my head.

"Luna," Elder Morris says, seeing me from the main house.

Everything inside tightens with anticipation. "Yes, Elder Morris?" I reply and walk toward him.

"What are you doing out so late?"

"I'm trying to find a bed."

"Any success?"

Shaking my head, I take a deep breath. "I haven't searched all the rooms yet."

"Come with me." He turns and leads me into one of the smaller houses. He opens a door to a bedroom, and he's met with giggles from some of my sisters. "Catherine," he commands one of the younger girls.

"Yes, Elder Morris?" she eagerly responds.

"Get up. You're sleeping with Lucille and Janet. Luna has your bed."

"Can't I just share with Luna?" she asks. More than just you and somebody else in the bed can get quite squashy.

"She can sleep with me," I say looking at Catherine. I don't want her to be moved just because of me.

"You have a bed to yourself. The others can share."

Catherine stands, and with her long nightdress, she quickly shuffles toward the bed with Lucille and Janet.

The fact I have a bed to myself will make the other girls hate me more. Why do the Elders have to do this? "Have a good sleep, Luna," Elder Morris says to me, before giving all my sisters a nod and backing out of the bedroom.

I'm met with glares. "Why are you so special?" Lucille asks. A chorus of agreement sounds behind her.

"It's always Luna, Luna, Luna. We can't talk to you, then we have to do everything you want us to. They even told us, tomorrow we're to do all your chores. Like Lucille asked, why are you so special?" Catherine huffs as she collapses into bed, obviously irritated with me.

"I don't know why the Elders are doing this." Yes, I do. It's to teach me a lesson. To make all my sisters hate me. "I'm sorry," I whisper. I lay on the bed, and turn so my back is to them. I don't want my sisters to see me crying.

"Go to sleep," Momma Edith's voice booms from the door.

Closing my eyes, I wish for it all to change. But I have a strong whirling feeling in my stomach that this is just the start of it.

Waking, I can feel the heat of the sun on my face. Opening my eyes, I look around the room and find it empty. The door is closed, but I can hear footsteps and hushed voices beyond the walls of the room.

I wished for this to be different, but as it's turning out, it's not. Catherine said they had to do my chores today, which is why I'm still in bed, alone. Everyone else would be awake, and preparing the meals. Serving the Elders. And doing what I would've been assigned.

My shoulders slump, and my stomach twists. I don't want to leave the room, but I know I have to.

Slowly, I tiptoe across the floor, steadying my shaky breath. I open the door, and listen for the voices closest to me. I can hear Momma Edith and Elder Steven talking. They're speaking in low voices. "The girl, what do you want me to do with her?" Momma Edith asks.

"Treat her like a princess."

What's a princess?

"What's the fascination with her?" Momma Edith's voice cracks, angrily. "It's as if she's something special."

"Do not speak to me like I'm one of the girls," Elder Steven says in a low voice. "I will remind you, under the conditions of our charter, I'm still an Elder, and you're merely a girl."

I can't see what's happening, but I'm picturing it in my mind. Elder Steven sounds angry, his low, tight voice sends shivers all the way through my body. It's like the way he gets when he's whipping me.

"I'm sorry, Steven," Momma Edith murmurs. She called him "Steven," not "Elder Steven." Except for the other Elders, I've never heard anyone call an Elder by their names.

"She's special. William says she's like none he's ever seen before."

"She's definitely not."

"You've been here from the start, have you ever seen anyone with so much spirit?"

"Not as long as we've been here. She's got more fight in her than any I've ever seen," Momma Edith says.

"Which is why it's important she doesn't know. And we nurture her to stay here. If she gets out, she has the power to bring this all down. Everything that's been created will be taken away."

"We can't have that happen."

My ears are echoing with so many words, and my curiosity is in overdrive. I want to run out and ask them what they're talking about. But I know, Elder Steven will whip me for listening.

Instead, I listen to more, but I hear another door open. If I'm caught, I'm going to be in so much trouble. Thinking as quickly as I can, I close the door to the room as quietly as I can, then open it loudly. Stepping out, I head in the direction of

Momma Edith and Elder Steven. I jump back when I see them, and place my hand to my chest. "You scared me," I say, trying to sound as normal as I can.

Momma Edith casts a wary gaze over me. Elder Steven smiles, and just then, Michael enters the room.

"Michael, what do you need?" Elder Steven asks.

"I'm hungry. Get me some food," Michael says to Momma Edith.

"Yes, Michael," she responds as she heads into the kitchen, Michael only a few steps behind her.

This leaves Elder Steven and me, alone in an awkward silence. He's staring at me, and I'm looking everywhere but at him. I can feel his intense glare. His eyes bore onto me. It makes my stomach roil with uneasiness. *He* makes me feel so uncomfortable.

"You'll be of age soon, Luna."

Bile quickly rises. "I know," I respond and try to keep the unease out of my voice.

"You'll be getting married."

Not if I can get out of here. "I know." I force a false smile on my face, but still refuse to look at him.

"Do you know who you'll be marrying?" The happiness in his voice means one thing, and one thing only. He's also made it obvious he wants me. *Him.*

I lower my gaze to look at my feet, then shake my head. Dread fills me, because I already know what he's going to say. "At this stage, it looks like it'll be me."

I'm not sure how to respond. Elder Steven has many wives, why would he want another? What am I supposed to say? Great? I can't wait? They'd all be a lie.

"I'm looking forward to our wedding night."

"Why?" I ask without thinking.

"Because I'll get to break in what's mine."

Huh? I don't understand the actual sentence. What do the words he just spoke, actually mean? *Breaking is bad, isn't it?*

CHAPTER NINE

THINGS HAVE SETTLED. Abigail still hates me, and Momma Kim, Momma Edith, Sister Janice, and Sister Holly continue to tell me how Abigail's being broken is my all fault.

The Elders are treating me the same. With extra attention.

Elder Steven is the worst. He's demanded I be the one to clean the floors in his bathroom. When I do, he stands behind me, and moans whenever I need to go on my knees to scrub them.

He makes my stomach stir with an uneasiness. The hair on the back of my neck always stands and my skin prickles. I'm hyperaware whenever he's near, and I always feel on edge with a hint of fear.

"Do you want to go?" Cain's voice snaps me out of my thought process. I look over to him, and notice he's indicating the wall with his head. I stop peeling the potatoes and smile.

"Go Luna," Sister Julie commands.

I offer her a small smile, but I know she's going to have to pick up the extra work of me leaving the potatoes behind. "I can stay."

"Once you've been wed, you'll have to learn how important it is to obey, not only your husband, but all the men."

"Do they have to obey us?" I ask, and internally scold myself. I should've kept my mouth shut.

Sister Julie lets out a laugh, as does Cain. I stare at him, silencing him with a mere glance. "We don't demand anything of the men. You know this. And, that question will earn you a whipping if you ask it again."

I look to Cain, and see the worry in his eyes. I bite on my tongue, feeling the metallic taste of blood inside my mouth. I want to know why the men won't obey *us*. I have so many questions, but obviously, I can't ask them. Not without consequence.

"Luna, let's go," Cain calls impatiently. His voice prompts me to turn and leave Sister Julie. The men speak, we obey. *How frustrating.*

I watch as Cain walks ahead of me. He keeps turning to make sure I'm following. I smile at him, as he smiles at me. But it doesn't take my mind off all the questions I have. Especially from the hole in the wall.

"Can we go this way?" I ask as I start moving in the direction of the hole.

"We can go anywhere you want," he calls back to me.

Funny, I really can't. Because I want to go beyond the wall, but I'm always told that's not an option. We keep walking, and find the spot where the hole is… or was. I don't know.

Cain falls to the ground. The sun shining down makes his honey-colored hair look longer than it actually is. "You need to ask Sister Lorraine to cut your hair," I say as I closely inspect the wall.

"Ask? I'll go tell her to do it."

"Cain." I turn to stare at him. "Don't be like them. Be different."

He looks at me, then down at the grass. Lifting his head, he watches me. "Sit." He points to the ground beside him.

"I want to stand." *And look where the hole is.* I take a few steps back, and turn to inspect the wall.

"What are you looking for?"

Bringing my hand up, I run it across the wall. It's cool to touch, and bumpy, but I can't feel any cracks where the wall can come down. Did I dream it all?

"Luna, what are you looking for?" Cain asks again, this time joining me on the search.

"I don't want to tell you, because you'll have to tell the Elders."

"I won't," he quickly responds.

This is bigger than me wanting to know about

what's beyond the wall. This is something so much more. "I can't," I say. My voice comes out pained. I want to, but I also don't want him to get in trouble.

"Luna, tell me," he encourages. I'm so scared of what can happen if he tells anyone.

"I can't," I say again. Tears brim my eyes, and although I want to, I know I can't. "Have you heard of a magazine?" I give him something.

"A what?"

"A magazine. Do you know what it is?" Cain shakes his head. "What about bourbon or M&M's?"

Cain shakes his head again. His lips downturn, as his eyes widen. "What are they?" I shrug. "Where did you hear those words."

I apparently didn't think this through properly. What do I say? I don't want to lie, but I obviously can't tell him the truth. "I dreamt them," I say, holding my breath for his reaction.

"You dreamt of words?"

"I dreamed of the Elders talking and they said those words. But, I didn't know what they were, so I asked them, and they whipped me." I'm so ashamed of myself. I really shouldn't be saying these lies. It's sinful. I can get whipped just because of the lies. But once the Elders hear them, they'll know I was listening.

"I don't know what they mean. Can't help you, Luna." I turn back, and keep looking for the crack in the wall. "But, I can help you find whatever it is you're looking for." He too closely inspects the wall, copying the way I'm looking for the crack. "What are we searching for?"

"It's nothing," I say again.

"Then why are we looking for nothing?"

I turn and lean my back against the wall, frustrated with myself. I know what I saw, but I have to find it. To prove it to myself, that I actually *did* see it. "Ugh," I grumble and take a few deep breaths.

"If you tell me what we're searching for, it'll make it much easier to find."

I can't. I really want to, but I can't. "It's nothing, don't worry about it." I turn and walk away, knowing if I keep looking Cain will continue to question what it is we're looking for. I'll have to come out here on my own. "I don't want to get married, Cain," I say trying to get him away from the wall.

"I know." He too turns, and comes to sit opposite me on the grass. "But, you have to." His features fall as he lowers his eyes. "I don't want you to get married either. Not to any of the Elders, I wish you could marry me."

My heart twists, and I'm faced with the reality of what's going to happen to me. I'm *going* to get married, but I don't want to. As much as I wish I could marry Cain instead of any of the Elders, I'm reconsidering that too. I'm not sure if that's what I want. What I really want is to find a way out from behind this wall, and discover what it's like outside.

"Luna?" Cain prompts me to answer him. "Don't you want to marry me too?"

I know what I have to say, but I'm not sure I feel it in my heart. "Yes." A severe ache stabs me in the chest. I lower my eyes, unable to look at Cain.

"Cain, you're needed," I hear Elder William calling.

Cain and I both stand, and look around us nervously. We weren't touching, we weren't doing anything wrong, so why we are both looking so worried I don't know.

"On my way." Cain turns and gives me a small smile as he walks away.

He's far away from us, and Elder William stands staring at me. He hasn't spoken, and I'm not brave enough to speak to him. "What are you doing out here, Luna?" Elder William asks.

"Cain and I were talking," I respond immediately. Already my mind is trying to make up a lie in case he asks what we were talking about.

"What were you discussing?"

I swallow hard. "About how I'll be married soon."

"How do you feel about that?" he asks.

I wasn't expecting to be asked something so

personal. Girls are married when we reach the age. I don't know if anyone's ever been asked how they feel about it. I shrug, unwilling to tell him that I don't want to marry Elder Steven, or anyone. Not yet. I don't know what the future holds. "It's what is expected," I reply in a small voice.

I notice Elder William's mouth twist in a smile. "But you don't want to get married?" he asks almost as if he can see inside my head and knows how I'm feeling.

I shrug again. I don't want to be whipped for my answer. "It's what's expected, Elder William. And if the Elders say it's time to marry, then I trust in my Elders to look after me." The words taste wrong. I don't believe them, but I'm hoping Elder William does.

"Do you want to know what's beyond the wall?"

I inhale sharply, excited. But I have to hide it. I know that my questions can earn me a whipping. "I'd like to know, but I also trust in my Elders."

"Death is outside." This is what we're always told. *Death, poverty, and disease.* "Death, poverty, and disease. Beyond the walls, it's dangerous. There are bad people out there, waiting to kill you. They will torture you. Tie you up, and beat you, then they'll hurt you in ways you can't even imagine. The people—I wouldn't even call them people, they're animals. They're very dangerous. What we have here…" He waves his hand around, showing me my home, "… in God's Haven, was made to keep you safe. You understand that, don't you, Luna?" I nod my head. I do understand how this is to keep me safe, but, I still want to see it all for myself. "You don't look too convinced."

"I am. And I'm so grateful to be safe." This is true. I am thankful I'm safe. But, how safe am I here? Always on the verge of a whipping for asking questions. Why can't I see what's happening beyond the wall? If it's as terrible as the Elders keep telling us, why don't they try and bring other people in here to save them too?

I have so many *whys* to ask. But I know I can't. Not without punishment from the Elders.

"You still don't look convinced."

Oh no, can he really tell? "I am." I smile. "So thankful I'm in here in Haven and not out there." I point to beyond the wall and scrunch my nose when I do so.

Elder William smiles at me. Hopefully I've convinced him. "I think you have some chores to do. Come, I'll walk back with you."

I want to stay here and keep searching the wall, but I'm forced to walk with Elder William. "I do have some chores."

"Elder Steven has requested you in the dining room."

Yuck. "Okay," I answer with as much happiness as I can raise.

"Elder Steven is very keen on you." I keep walking, turn, and smile as I move forward. Elder

William walks slow, and I want to walk as fast as possible to get away from him. The fact he's brought up Elder Steven makes my skin tighten with worry. "You know, Luna, there are a few of the Elders who want to take you as their bride."

"Oh," I reply and add a smile. It's not a real smile, I just have to make sure none of my reactions can earn me a whipping.

"You've been our most popular girl yet."

I don't even know what that means. And I don't want to know either. "Oh."

"Elder Steven is looking forward to his wedding night. He won't share you with any of us yet."

"I'm not sure what you mean." I know the Sisters have told me he'll put his penis in my vagina, and I'll have to do that with any of the Elders who want to put their penis inside me, but I'm not sure what Elder William means by sharing.

"When we get back, go to Momma Edith and ask her to explain your duties once you're a bride. It's a little bit different as to what it is before you're married. Being married is a privilege. No other girl has had as much interest as you have." I can tell by the way he's speaking, I'm supposed to feel special. But I don't *want* to feel special. I want them to *not* want me. "It's a rite of passage for the girls. Do you know, some girls aren't even wanted? The Elders are very selective as to who they take as their brides. Once they've picked, the bride is protected for eternity."

Except for Theresa, I heard she wasn't protected. She couldn't bear children, so she was sent away. I want to be sent away too. "I know," I say.

"And you, Luna, are so lucky." He keeps telling me this, as if he's trying to convince me. "So many of the Elders want you," he repeats.

"Thank you. It's an honor." I offer him a smile, as genuine as I can. "I have chores, I should tend to them."

"Yes, yes. Off you go."

I don't wait for Elder William to say anything else. Instead, I pick up my pace and walk ahead of him back to the main house. Sister Julie is still peeling the potatoes, and Momma Kim is sitting behind her, having a drink. I notice how many more potatoes Sister Julie has to peel. I feel bad that I left her, so I walk over to her and help.

"Nice of you to finally join us," Momma Kim says in an icy cold voice.

"Sorry, Momma Kim. Cain wanted me."

"Oh, then that's acceptable." She gives me a small nod, then pointedly looks at the stack of potatoes. "You better hurry up. Elder Steven wants you in the dining room tonight."

"Yes, Momma."

The potatoes are peeled in silence. Sister Julie goes on to prepare the beans. I help her, and

Momma Kim still sits watching us, not offering to help. There's a tightness in the room. It's almost hard to breathe in here. I can feel Momma Kim's eyes on me. But I don't dare turn to look at her.

I once thought Momma Kim was nicer than Momma Edith, but right now, I think she may be just as scary, if not worse than Momma Edith.

The worst thing is, I don't know what I've done to have her fury focused on me.

CHAPTER TEN

WAKING IN DARKNESS is normal for me. I always have so many chores to tend to, so, like the other girls, we wake before the sun has risen and start with the chores.

The Elders eat, then the men need to eat. We all have certain jobs to do. It seems I've been on dining duty more than the other girls, which I don't like. Because I find Elder Steven always being too nice to me, and not so pleasant to whoever I'm with.

This makes the other girls not like me.

"Luna, I need you to go and get the eggs," Sister Helen instructs.

"Okay," I reply, take the basket and head out toward the chicken coop.

As I walk out, I look around me. The wall disappears behind the trees where they say it's diseased and if anyone goes there, they'll die.

Something about it makes me more curious. If the trees are diseased, then why do they look so healthy? Wouldn't the disease be making its way closer to us? Wouldn't the Elders try to protect us from it? Is that why they tell us to not go near the trees?

I find myself passing by the chickens, and walking toward the trees. I want to see them for myself. I know beyond the wall there is death, but there's nothing like that inside the wall.

Reaching the edge of the trees, I look up at them. They're giant, so big. I've never really noticed how big they actually are. Looking into the huge stand of trees, I notice how dark it is in there. Turning, I see the sun is rising, and it's not so dark, but inside the trees, it's almost like it was when I woke.

I take a hesitant step in, not sure what I'm doing. My heart pounds inside my chest. I want to see the dying trees. I know I can't see what's beyond the wall, but I can see this. I want to know what diseased trees look like. I won't touch them, just in case they are sick, but I still want to see them for myself.

I slow my steps as I creep further into the depth of the trees. The trees grow denser. The light from the sun is getting fainter, the darkness is growing thicker. I turn back and see it's light beyond the trees. I can see the main house in the far distance, but as I keep walking, the house becomes smaller.

"Just look for the sick trees, then return," I say

to myself.

I turn to look at the main house. It's so small I can barely make it out. The trees are tall, and stand thick together. Looking up, I'm covered in a shelter of thick leaves so high up, I can't make anything else out.

But, I keep walking. I want to see.

Beneath my shoes, the ground is moist and springy. I lean down and touch the land. It's wet and so cold. "Wow," I whisper at the amazing feel on my fingertips. This gives me courage to keep walking.

But when I do turn back again, this time I can't see the main house. Even though my heart has calmed, I'm still scared of what I'll find. What if I can't find my way home? What if I touch a tree that's diseased, and I die out here?

I've come this far, I have to keep going.

A noise startles me. It sounds like footsteps. I freeze in fear. Is something going to hurt me? I hold my breath, hoping whatever *it* is, doesn't see me and moves away. As the noise creeps closer, my heart beats wildly. The blood in my veins quickens, and my eyes widen with fear and terror.

I can't help but not move. I'm completely terrified. Is this where death is?

Will I die here? Out among the trees where no one comes because the trees are diseased?

The crunching of the dried leaves on the ground stops.

I try and calm my erratic breath as I turn my head in the direction of the sound. If I'm going to die, I'm going to die looking at whatever it is about to kill me.

Nothing appears, I'm still stuck on the spot. Waiting...

Suddenly, from behind a tree, an animal appears, steps forward, lowers its head and grazes on the leaves that have fallen from the tall trees.

"Oh my," I say as I let out a deep breath. The animal is something I've not seen before. "You scared me," I say softly as I approach it.

The animal lifts its head, and stares at me as I step toward it. I know from the chickens and cows we have at home, they wander toward us, especially when we have buckets of food for them. This one doesn't move toward me. It stops eating, eyes carefully watching me as I walk slowly toward it.

"It's okay, I won't hurt you," I say as I lift my hand so I can touch it.

The animal backs away from me slowly. It's a peculiar looking animal, with a small head, and small pointy ears. Its body is round, and it has splotches on its skin.

"I won't hurt you," I say again in a smaller voice hoping it'll let me pat it.

But the animal turns and scrambles away from me.

"I'm sorry," I call after it. I interrupted its

eating; hopefully it'll find something else to graze on.

My erratic heartbeat is now calm, I'm not as scared as I was. I thought something was going to hurt me, but as it turns out, it was only an animal who was looking for something to eat. Thankfully, that something wasn't me.

I keep walking, and the trees become thicker and bigger. I avoid touching them because of their disease. It also becomes colder and darker as I enter further into the trees.

"Where's the wall?" I ask myself as I turn to search for it. But I can't see it. I know I would've reached it by now, but I haven't yet. Maybe the trees have made it diseased. Maybe it's broken away and there's nothing left of it.

Something inside me shifts.

I'm happy and worried at the same time.

If there's no wall, that means I can go beyond. But if there's no wall, then that means, the tortured souls beyond can also make their way in. I'm not sure which is more terrifying.

The thought I can get out, or that death and illness can get in.

I want to see what's beyond the wall. I know I can get hurt, or die, but I need to see it for myself. If what they say is true and I make it back in, then I'll be able to understand what the Elders keep telling us. I'll never question what they say again, but I *need* to see it for myself.

The trees are now thick and dense, I can barely walk through them without touching. It's so dark, I need to let my eyes adjust to the lack of the light. I walk slowly, and carefully in the same direction, hoping to reach the other side soon.

It doesn't seem too long, before I come across wires. The wires reach from the ground upward, and look like they travel for a long way across and behind the trees. There's a big sign on them, but I can't read so I'm not sure what they say.

I stare at the words. Sounding them out like Cain has taught me.

"C-a-u-t-i-o-n. Caowteeeyeohn. What does Cawoteeyeohn mean?" I say aloud. There's more words, still unsure what they say. Eeleekt-t-treek fenk-k-k-ee." I'm trying really hard to understand what it's supposed to say, but I'm struggling. I say it again, fast, in case it makes better sense.

"Cawoteeyeohn. Eeleekt-t-treek fenk-k-k-ee." Frustrated with myself, I say it again. "Cawoteeyeohn. Eeleekt-t-treek fenk-k-k-ee." Why can't I read? Because the Elders say girls don't need to. How frustrating.

I have no idea what the words say. All I know is I need to get on the other side of the wires.

Lifting my hand, I warily reach toward the wires.

The sign is old and weathered, but I know it's meant to be there for a reason. But, I want to see what's on the other side.

I need to get out.

My fingers are so close to the wires. Slowly, I extend my hand, stretching to touch them. I close one eye and lift my shoulders, waiting for something to happen. I reach further, until my finger is nearly touching.

If this is going to kill me, then at least I can say I tried.

My finger touches the wire. I wait for something to happen.

Nothing does.

"Oh," I say. I look to the rough sign with faded words and tilt my head. "I thought you meant something important." I giggle to myself.

"Now, how do I get past you?" I ask the wires.

I look both ways and decide to follow the wires for as long as I can before I'm back inside behind the wall. The wall is nowhere. I can't even see it from here. I know I'm past it, so these wires must end somewhere.

Following the wires leads me to a door. There's another sign on the door, and I don't know what it says. The door has a simple latch, like the bedrooms of the Elders. Elder Steven has a special latch on a door in his bedroom. It's got a round part at the top, and I've seen him use a special metal pin he puts in it. He once told me it's called a kay, or key. I can't remember. He told me he has special things inside that room, and that room is only for him to use with his wives. I don't know what he meant then, I still have no idea now. All I know, is he has a special latch on his door, much like the one I'm seeing here.

"How do I open you?" I ask the latch, but don't really expect an answer. The door is made out of the same wire as the fence, but thicker.

"Maybe the key is here." I look on the ground, kick some of the leaves with my feet to see if it's fallen. "That wouldn't be very smart, would it, Luna? If death is out there, they're not going to leave a kay in the latch so anyone can come in." I slap my forehead and roll my eyes at my own dumbness.

Looking up at the wires, there's round wires on top of them, they have spiky parts sticking out, so climbing is not going to happen. The spiky parts look like they'd hurt. "This can't be it." I walk further down. "I can't reach here, and not be able to go any further." I kick the bottom of the wire in anger.

It lifts off the ground.

"What?" I gasp and step back, looking at how the wire is not straight down, but dented out where I kicked it. I kick it again.

The wire vibrates, but I make a bigger hole at the bottom.

I look around me, to make sure no one is watching, and I kick it again, and again. "I think I can fit through."

Getting on the ground, I try to fit my head

through, but my hair gets caught in the wire. "It needs to be bigger, Luna." I wiggle back, and rip some hair off my head. "Ouch." I cry as I rub the spot it's been ripped out of.

I get up off the ground, and walk around trying to work out how I'm going to get through.

"Okay," I say to myself. I bring both my hands up to my head and place them on either side of my head. Then, I move them to my shoulders, where I notice my shoulders are wider than my head. I keep them as wide as my shoulders, and run them down my body. When I get to my feet, I know the widest part is my shoulders. I need to be able to get my shoulders through the hole. If I can't get them through, I won't be able to get the rest of me out either.

"You can do this, Luna." I get on my hands and knees, and start digging the hole out to be as wide as I can. Dirt is getting beneath my nails, and something pricks my hand. "Ouch," I say as I lift is and notice a small cut on my palm. "Keep going." Determined to see what's beyond the wall, I keep digging—leaving the pain of the cut on my hand behind.

I can do this.

I *can.*

The more I dig, the larger the hole gets. Thinking it's deep enough, I try to get through it. I make it further than before, but my shoulders are still too wide for the little hole. I back out, and dig furiously knowing I have more to go before I can fit through.

When the hole looks bigger, I squeeze under it.

My head crosses the wire fence, then I pause. I bring my shoulders under, and they manage to fit, only just.

Then I use my arms to drag myself out to the other side.

When my feet are through, I lie on the ground, smiling. I got out. I made it out, and I did it by myself. With no help.

But the scary realization sets in quite quickly. Now what?

Now I'm about to go *out there,* and see all the death and disease. Am I really ready for this?

I take some long, deep breaths and try to convince myself not to go and discover what it's like. But, even to myself, I know if I don't do this, I'll regret every moment. "You're out here, Luna, what's the worst thing that can happen?"

"You can die," I answer myself.

"The worst thing is you won't know what it's actually like. Go see it for yourself," I reply to myself.

My brain is conflicted. I want to go, but I'm terrified of what I'll find.

"You can do this, Luna." I pull my shoulders back, and head in the direction of disease and death.

CHAPTER ELEVEN

I'VE BEEN WALKING for a while, and I'm still in the thick of the trees. They don't seem to become any thinner. My feet are hurting, but my determination spurs me on.

Suddenly, I come to the edge of the trees. Beyond the trees, is nothing. Just land as far as I can see.

It's like the trees completely disappear. The sun has left, and now the moon has come out. I must've been walking a while. My tummy grumbles, and it reminds me how I haven't eaten.

But I'm mostly thirsty.

Standing at the edge of the trees, I try to work out which way to go. There really is nothing here. The darkness of the night doesn't let me see clearly, but it's also quiet. Maybe the tortured souls have all died. Maybe there's no life beyond the wall.

I should turn back.

Go back to where I know I'm safe.

Don't stop now.

I either keep going, or I turn back. But, I've come this far.

My feet and heart know what to do. They keep moving forward, in the darkness.

As I'm moving, I notice how the quiet is replaced by many sounds. Something between mumbling, and laughter, and even moaning. I squint to see ahead of me, a fire is burning. As I approach the fire, everything becomes clearer. There are pieces of material held up by poles everywhere.

"Hey, watch where you're going!" a rough male voice growls at me as I step on something.

"I'm sorry," I reply, but can't see who yelled at me.

My eyes are focused, and I'm searching for something, but I don't know what I'm actually looking for. "You don't look like you belong here," the same deep voice says as he stands. He's a man. A very tall man. Much like Elder Steven. But he's very dirty, and when he smiles, his teeth are all rotten.

"Are you diseased?" I ask. My voice is just above a whisper.

"Diseased? What are you talking about, woman?" he snarls as he looks me up and down.

"Woman? What's a woman?" I ask.

He tilts his head in question and steps forward. I step back, because if he's diseased, then I don't want to get sick too. Automatically, I raise my hand to cover my mouth and nose. I need to get back, I shouldn't be here. Trembling with fear, I begin to run. But I running away from the wall, not toward it.

The diseased and tortured are getting thicker and thicker. I run through them, hoping I haven't caught what they have.

As I'm running, I hit into a wall. But it's not a wall, it's a man. "Hey, sugar, slow down."

Stepping back, I look up at him. "You're not diseased?" I ask as I take in his healthy appearance.

"Diseased? What are you talking about?"

"Are you an Elder?"

He looks me up and down, a small questioning look on his face. "An Elder?" He shakes his head in response. "Where are you from?" I point behind me. He looks over my shoulder to where I'm pointing, then asks, "How long have you been on the streets?"

"On the what?" It's like he's talking words I don't understand.

"How old are you?" He steps forward, I step back. I look him up and down, like he did to me and notice his clothing is clean. His teeth aren't the same color as the other man's. His teeth are like mine. "You look lost. Just wait here, I'm going to get my supervisor." He steps back and away from me, then brings his hand up to scratch at his chin. "Actually, I think you should come with me." He takes a cautious look around him.

"If you're diseased, I'm not going anywhere with you." I step back again, this time stepping on something.

"Watch out!" I hear a girl yell.

"Sorry," I quickly reply.

The man who's clean watches me. "Okay, don't come with me, but promise me you'll stay here." He lifts both his hands and makes a stop gesture with them. "I'll be right back with my supervisor."

"What's a supervisor?" I ask in a small voice when he leaves.

I stand in the spot the man told me to, and look around. Everyone but the man are so dirty. It smells here too. Like the bathrooms back at the houses. They smell really bad.

"Luna!" I hear a voice. A voice I know all too well.

Turning slowly, I see the eyes of the Elder I know will beat me.

"Elder Steven," I say as I lower my head but keep my gaze on him.

He walks angrily toward me, grabs me by my upper arm, and pulls me away from all the disease. He drags me back to where I came from. Back toward the thick trees. Back toward the darkness. Back behind the wall.

"What the hell do you think you're doing?"

"I…"

I don't get to answer. Instead, something sharp is jabbed into me, and before I know it, everything turns black. Am I diseased now too? Am I a tortured soul? Am I dead?

CHAPTER TWELVE

I OPEN MY eyes, and blink several times trying to focus.

I try to move my arms, but they're stuck.

Panic fills me. My wrists are tied to the wall with heavy chains. I'm kneeling, and hurting. "Hello!" I yell. "Where am I?" My heart rate is at an all-time high. I've never felt so scared. Not even when…

Wait, did I make it beyond the wall? Did I really see all the diseased? Am I dead? Is this where the dead go? Do we become chained to the wall? Why am I alone? Are there others?

"Help!" I scream even louder.

"Luna," Elder Steven enters the room from a door opposite to where I'm kneeling. My knees are blistering in hot pain, and my back is protesting too.

"Why am I here? Why can't I move?" I ask as I

try to tug at the chains around my wrists.

Elder Steven shakes his head at me. His mouth is pressed into a thin, angry line. "Why did you leave, Luna?" His voice is low, reminding me of the time he caught Cain trying to teach me to read.

"I..I…" I stumble with my words. I'm not too sure what I can say that won't earn me a whipping. But, I'm also bound by chains to hooks on the wall, unable to move. I think a whipping is the least of my worries.

Elder Steven walks toward me. He comes to stand in front of me. Because I'm kneeling, he towers over me. The tops of his legs are at my eye-level. "Don't lie to me, Luna. I don't like girls who lie." He reaches out, and gently strokes my chin. I move my head away, because I know, he's not gentle. He's horrible and mean.

I can't help but notice there are no windows in here. "Where am I?" I ask, still looking everywhere but at Elder Steven.

"You're home, Luna."

"I've never seen this room."

Elder Steven laughs. "This is my room of *enjoyment*," he says in a whisper. The hair on my arms raises, and my skin crawls when he says the word 'enjoyment.' "Do you want to see what I find enjoyable?"

No, I don't. I can't seem to find my voice. All I can do is shake my head.

The shock of what happens next startles me at

first, then blinding pain screams at me. My cheek feels like it's exploding with hot coals from an open fire. "No!" I cry as the pain rips through my head.

"Yes," he murmurs, and hits me on the side. The pain is matching. Matching and intolerable.

"Stop!" I cry louder. "Help me."

"No one can hear you in here, Luna. This room is specially designed so I can have my fun without disturbing anyone. Aren't you having fun? I am."

He smacks me again, and this time my cheek feels like it's shattered. "Why are you doing this?" I try and escape, but I'm restrained and I can't even shelter my head from the blows.

"Tell me you're having fun." He hits me again.

The impact of this strike makes me bite the inside of my cheek. There is a metallic taste in my mouth. The blows to my face are screwing with my head. The pain is like a pounding headache that doesn't let up. "Stop!" I plead with him.

He stops, and paces in front of me. "You should know, Luna, I don't like it when girls try to run away."

"I wasn't," I instantly respond. "I just wanted to see what it was like out there."

"Don't lie," he angrily shouts, then adds another slap to the side of my head. This one makes me dizzy. "Why were you trying to run away? Don't we give you the world here?"

The world? The world? I look up at him. "The

world?" I ask. He stares down at me, and his eyes widen, as if I've caught him doing something he shouldn't. "There's more beyond the wall?"

He blinks at me. Caught. But he quickly morphs into angry Elder Steven again. "No, there's nothing out there." He lays a swift kick into my stomach.

I try to double over in pain, but the chains won't let me. The kick to my stomach winds me, and I try to drag air into my lungs. But everything inside my chest is burning in agony. "There's more, isn't there?" He hits me on the side of the head. But I refuse to give up. I want to know. "Tell me." Another kick to my stomach.

My body is refusing to co-operate. It's giving up. But I will *not* die without knowing the truth.

"We are your world. Your universe. Your everything."

Smack.

"TELL ME!" I yell through gritted teeth. "There's more beyond the wall, isn't there?"

Smack. "We are your world." Smack. Kick.

As Elder Steven continues the beating, the door creaks open, and Elder William enters. "Enough, Steven," he says. Elder Steven turns, smirks at him, then hits me again. "She's just a child. That's enough," Elder William says more sternly.

"She broke the rules."

"She's a child. You can do what you want with her once she becomes your bride."

"I'm not marrying him," I say loud enough for them both to hear. My body is hurting. My wrists are burning in pain from where I'm tied, my stomach aches from the kicks, and my eyes are swelling shut.

"It's cute you think you have a choice," Elder Steven replies.

"Steven," Elder William snaps. "Go." He pointedly looks toward the door.

Elder Steven steps back from me, then spits on the floor right by my knee. He moves his thumb, and wipes the spittle from his lips. "You and I are not done. Not yet." Turning, he leaves the room. The thick door to the room closes, making a soft noise as it latches shut.

"Luna, why did you leave?" Elder William asks in a gentle voice.

I tilt my head at him so I can see him out of the slits my swollen eyes have become. He's being nice to me, but an Elder who can watch another beat someone can't be nice at all. It's all lies. Everything they are is a lie. I shake my head at him. "What does it matter?" I try to shrug, but the blazing sting makes me whimper in pain.

"It matters to me," he says.

"Why?" Although I'm the one restrained, I still feel strong. I know something they don't want me to know. I know there's more than they've been telling us.

"Because I need to know the knowledge you

have, about…" he pauses and walks around the small room, then stops near the door before finishing, "… outside."

So many things go through my head. I'm dangerous. I know something he's desperately tried to keep from us. I just need to work out what that *something* is.

"It doesn't matter," I say again, this time stronger than before. But a thought enters my mind, and I can't help but to ask. I narrow my eyes and tilt my head.

I see the worry on Elder William's face. "What?" he asks, his tone filled with bother.

"How did you find me?"

He smiles, and steps back from me. "When we realized, you were missing, we knew you had found your way out. And we knew, the diseased trees wouldn't have kept you in. Elder Steven went looking for you. He found the hole you dug, and knew you were gone. He figured out how you got out, and went searching for you. He was close behind, close enough to get to you before anyone even realized you were out." I shake my head at myself. I was careless. That won't ever happen again. "I was honest with you Luna, now I need to know, what *you* know about the outside."

I shake my head again. I'm not telling him anything. The silence is deafening. My body shakes with anger, but I will *not* tell him what he wants to know.

"You leave us no choice, Luna." He leaves through the door. In less than a heartbeat, a sound comes from somewhere.

"We are your family. Beyond the wall is death. Beyond the wall is evil. You will die if you leave. Only we can protect you," the female voice chants.

"Hello?" I call.

"We are your family. Beyond the wall is death. Beyond the wall is evil. You will die if you leave. Only we can protect you."

"Who are you?" I can't place the voice. It doesn't sound like anyone I know.

"We are your family. Beyond the wall is death. Beyond the wall is evil. You will die if you leave. Only we can protect you."

I listen to the voice. It's the same every time she speaks, the same words. It's deadly even, with no emotion in it.

"We are your family. Beyond the wall is death. Beyond the wall is evil. You will die if you leave. Only we can protect you."

"Hello?" I say in a smaller voice.

"We are your family. Beyond the wall is death. Beyond the wall is evil. You will die if you leave. Only we can protect you. We are your family. Beyond the wall is death. Beyond the wall is evil. You will die if you leave. Only we can protect you. We are your family. Beyond the wall is death. Beyond the wall is evil. You will die if you leave. Only we can protect you. We are your family.

Beyond the wall is death. Beyond the wall is evil. You will die if you leave. Only we can protect you.

"STOP!" I scream.

The same voice continues. Over and over and over again. It's messing with my head, and I hate the voice. It's so… lifeless.

"We are your family. Beyond the wall is death. Beyond the wall is evil. You will die if you leave. Only we can protect you. We are your family. Beyond the wall is death. Beyond the wall is evil. You will die if you leave. Only we can protect you. We are your family. Beyond the wall is death. Beyond the wall is evil. You will die if you leave. Only we can protect you. We are your family. Beyond the wall is death. Beyond the wall is evil. You will die if you leave. Only we can protect you. We are your family. Beyond the wall is death. Beyond the wall is evil. You will die if you leave. Only we can protect you.

"STOP!" I yell again.

"We are your family. Beyond the wall is death. Beyond the wall is evil. You will die if you leave. Only we can protect you.."

I don't know how much longer the voice keeps saying the same thing.

My head is pounding. My body is aching. And I can't move.

"We are your family. Beyond the wall is death. Beyond the wall is evil. You will die if you leave. Only we can protect you. We are your family.

Beyond the wall is death. Beyond the wall is evil. You will die if you leave. Only we can protect you."

Eventually my eyes drift closed, and a curtain of darkness falls over me.

The female voice is close. It doesn't stop. The words don't stop, "We are your family. Beyond the wall is death. Beyond the wall is evil. You will die if you leave. Only we can protect you."

We are your family.

Beyond the wall is death.

Beyond the wall is evil.

You will die if you leave.

Only we can protect you.

If this is protecting me, I don't want it.

CHAPTER THIRTEEN

MY EYES OPEN. My body is throbbing. The voice is still playing, still reciting the same words. I try to turn, but now, even my neck is sore.

"You're awake," another voice says. *Elder Steven.* "I was worried."

I search for him, but can't see where he is. My vision is blurry, it's difficult to focus because I can barely open my eyes. His work. "Worried?" I chuckle. "That's why you have me here. Tied? Because you're worried about me?"

"You haven't been listening, have you? We are your family. Beyond the wall is death. Beyond the wall is evil. You will die if you leave. Only we can protect you," he repeats the words with confidence.

"Sounds like you believe the words."

"You'll learn to believe them too. You just need extra convincing. And this is why I like you so much, Luna. You have fire and spirit, and I want to be the one who breaks it out of you." He comes into view, standing tall before me.

"Is that the enjoyment you told me about? You like to *break* girls?" Although I still don't know exactly what that means, I'm quickly learning to interpret what he's saying. There's another meaning to break, I'm just not sure *what* it means yet. He tried to break me with the punches, kicks and slaps.

"I've never met anyone like you before." He grabs my chin in his hand, and rubs his thumb over my lip. "And you'll learn exactly how much enjoyment I will take from you."

"Why wait? Why don't you take your enjoyment from me now?"

He laughs. "Believe me, I've thought about it. But William would have my head if I touch you before you come of age."

The more he talks, the more questions I have. But I can barely keep my head up from all the pain. "I'm hungry," I say.

"You think I'm going to feed you? That's not going to happen. Not until you admit, we are your family. Beyond the wall is death. Beyond the wall is evil. You will die if you leave. Only we can protect you."

I smirk. "Is that what you want to hear?" I feel the strength inside me increasing.

"I want you to believe it."

"Then you'll be waiting for many moons," I retort.

"And you'll be hungry."

I glare at him the best I can. "I'd rather die."

Elder Steven's eyes narrow at me. A muscle in his neck tenses, and his hands become fists. He takes a breath, and steps backward until his back is against the wall. "I can arrange that, too. Truthfully, I'd enjoy it."

"Why are you doing this?" I ask.

"Because you need to learn we are your family."

I shake my head. "No. Family doesn't do this to each other." I rattle the chains, indicating how I'm shackled. "You're not my family." *You never will be.*

A slow grin pulls at his lips. "Oh yes, I'm going to enjoy this very much." With those words, he leaves the room.

The voice starts again.

"We are your family. Beyond the wall is death. Beyond the wall is evil. You will die if you leave. Only we can protect you."

Elder Steven's smirk worries me. I know something's going to happen. I'm not entirely sure on what that something is, but I have an awful feeling I won't have to wait for long.

The voice continues.

"We are your family. Beyond the wall is death.

Beyond the wall is evil. You will die if you leave. Only we can protect you."

My stomach churns with a combination of worry and hunger; they compete with each other. Both are strong, but I think worry may be a stronger reaction than hunger.

"Help!" I try to scream, but my throat is too dry. I have a feeling screaming and yelling won't achieve anything. I can't imagine the Elders have brought me to a place where someone can hear me, and come in to help me. I'm somewhere they can do what they want with me, and no one will know anything about it.

It makes me think. How many others have they done this to? How many haven't made it out alive?

"We are your family. Beyond the wall is death. Beyond the wall is evil. You will die if you leave. Only we can protect you."

The door opens.

Elder William walks in first, and holds the door open.

There's a repetitive sound I can hear above the voice, a squeaking noise. "Are you sure?" Elder William asks.

It doesn't take too long to see where the squeaky sound is coming from. There's a bathtub on wheels being pushed into the room. Water sloshes up the edges and out of the bath, splashing to the floor. Elder Steven pushes it into the room.

I feel my forehead crinkle in question. He's

going to give me a bath? But the tub is high up off the floor. How am I supposed to get in it?

"I'm sure," Elder Steven replies and gives Elder William a wink and a smile. Though both seem quite sinister. Maybe, this *isn't* a bath.

Behind him, Momma Edith enters carrying a bucket in each hand, and pours them into the bath. She looks at me, frowns, and shakes her head. "We are your family," she says. "Remember this. Only we can protect you." She leaves and Elder William follows.

Before Elder William closes the door, he says to Elder Steven, "Don't take it too far."

Momma Edith enters with the same buckets, and empties them again. She leaves quickly without even glancing at me.

I flick my gaze back to Elder Steven who's standing in front of me, smiling. "I won't. She just needs to learn. When she understands, I'll stop."

"She's still a child."

"She'll be legal soon. And no one even knows she's here."

"Just don't take it too far," Elder William says again, in a lower, more serious voice.

"I won't."

Elder William departs the room. The door closing behind him.

Now, I'm terrified. I'm not sure what's going to happen. The look on Elder Steven's face tells me he's going to enjoy it, which means I won't.

"You know, Luna. I think we're way past the Elder-girl relationship now."

I squint. What does he mean? I don't dare ask.

"I'm going to untie you." He walks to my side, produces something small and silver, and unlocks the shackles on my wrists, then steps around and repeats it on the other side. I rub at my wrists where the cuffs cut into me, and notice the angry red, circular marks. "But this, this is going to be the highlight of my year."

He lifts me by my shoulders. My legs cramp from being on my knees for so long. "My legs," I cry as I try to massage the back of them. I can barely feel my feet. They tingle as I try to stand.

"Your legs will be the least of your worries soon." He grabs the back of my neck, squeezes, and pulls me along to the bath. He dunks my head into the water, I try to scream and fight him. As I inhale, I take in water, unable to catch my breath because my head is held under.

He lifts my head, and I try to suck air into my lungs. "Stop!" I manage to splutter.

The voice plays in the background. "We are your family. Beyond the wall is death. Beyond the wall is evil. You will die if you leave. Only we can protect you."

He dunks my head straight under the water again. I barely got the chance to get air into my lungs. I'm trying to fight him, clawing at his arms to let me up. I try to scream again, but I'm only taking in more water. My body is in agony, my chest is exploding with fire and sizzling pain.

He lifts my head, leans down and whispers, "We are your family. Beyond the wall is death. Beyond the wall is evil. You will die if you leave. Only we can protect you."

"No, you're not! Family doesn't do this."

He chuckles, then adds, "You're a hard one to break." Then quickly submerges my head again under the water. I try to fight him again. But I feel his other hand come up to the back of my head, holding me under.

The words are loud, and I can still hear them. But the panic inside my body is enough to fuel me to hold strong. "We are (*not*) your family. Beyond the wall is (*life not*) death. Beyond the wall is (*good and not*) evil. You will die (*live*) if you leave. Only we can (*won't*) protect you."

He lifts my head. I try to breathe in, knowing what he's going to continue doing. I save my words and strength, it's no use fighting with him. Not when he's got control over me just by his mere size and power.

"We are your family. Beyond the wall is death. Beyond the wall is evil. You will die if you leave. Only we can protect you," he says. I shake my head, not believing him. "Again?" he asks.

"No more!" I whimper. My head is so wet, I don't even know if I'm crying or not.

"See, this is fun." He pushes my head down again.

I flail and fight. But the longer he holds my head under, the more my body loses its will to fight. My arms become less frantic. My heart slows. My skin is bursting with pain.

He pulls me up out of the water. "We are your family. Beyond the wall is death. Beyond the wall is evil. You will die if you leave. Only we can protect you."

"No," I say in a small voice.

"You're not learning, Luna." He shoves my head under again.

This time I make the decision. They want to hear those words from me. I will repeat the words. But I refuse to believe them. They can break my body, they can break my bones, but they will *not* break my will.

He pulls me up, and in a small, tired voice I say, "We are your family. Beyond the wall is death. Beyond the wall is evil. You will die if you leave. Only we can protect you."

"What? Say it louder, Luna."

I can barely stand; every part of my body is hurting. But I muster the strength to say what I need to so he'll stop. "We are your family. Beyond the wall is death. Beyond the wall is evil. You will die if you leave. Only we can protect you."

"Now, I think you're saying it to stop this." He forces my head under once again.

I have no fight left in my body.

The fight I have, is only in my mind.

I don't even bother trying to swing my arms anymore. He's going to continue this, regardless of what I say and do. He brings my head up, but he's still got his hand around my neck squeezing so hard it hurts.

"We are your family. Beyond the wall is death. Beyond the wall is evil. You will die if you leave. Only we can protect you," I say as I cough and splutter though it. His hand eases, and he steps back from me. I fall to a heap on the floor, barely able to support my own body weight. I repeat, "We are your family. Beyond the wall is death. Beyond the wall is evil. You will die if you leave. Only we can protect you." This time, I let tears fall.

Elder Steven's shoes go out of view. The floor is wet, and I don't care that I'm sitting in water. My breath heaves in and out, trying to get air into my body.

"Good," he says, and knocks twice on the door.

The door opens instantly, Elder Steven takes the bath on wheels away, pulling it out of the room. The door closes again, this time, I'm left alone.

I lay on the cold, wet floor for a long time.

The voice repeats the same words, over and over again. "We are your family. Beyond the wall is death. Beyond the wall is evil. You will die if you leave. Only we can protect you."

No, they're not my family.

Beyond the wall is more.

Beyond the wall there may be evil, but there's evil inside the wall too.

They will not protect me.

I shiver on the icy floor. My clothes are soaked through to my skin. My eyes can barely open because of the swelling.

But I make a silent promise to myself.

I will escape from here. I will escape, and go beyond the wall.

CHAPTER FOURTEEN

"HOW ARE YOU today, Luna?" Elder Steven asks.

The voice hasn't stopped. But I have to put on a brave front. They need to think I'm like them now.

"I'm fine, Elder Steven."

"Your eyes are looking better."

I pull myself up off the floor, and lower my head as he enters the small room. I'm not sure how long I've been here, but I know there must've been a lot of sunrises. There's a bucket in the corner, which I use as a bathroom. And Elder Steven brings me food. Not a lot, but there's some. "Thank you," I say in a small voice.

The voice continues saying the same thing, over and over again. "We are your family. Beyond the wall is death. Beyond the wall is evil. You will die if you leave. Only we can protect you."

"How are you feeling?" The question is loaded. If I say I hate him, he'll bring in the bath and dunk my head in water again. If I say I'm fine, then he'll be suspicious of that too. Either way, he won't believe me.

I opt for the safest one. "I don't like being in here. But I'm okay. And I'm hungry." I rub my hand across my stomach. I can feel how my stomach has sunken in, and I know it's because I haven't been eating.

"Soon, I think you'll be ready to be re-introduced into our society."

I frown at him. "Has anyone asked about me?"

"Anyone in particular?" He leans against the back of the door, reminding me how I can't get out until he allows me.

"Has Cain asked?"

Elder Steven smiles. The way he draws his lips up, slowly, and intentional, warns on how horrible he actually is. "No," he answers after a brief hesitation.

I want to bite back, to challenge him. But I also know the treatment I can expect if I do. And this time he may not stop until he drowns me.

"We are your family. Beyond the wall is death. Beyond the wall is evil. You will die if you leave. Only we can protect you." The words irritate me. They annoy me. Other than Elder Steven, it's the only thing to keep me company while I'm stuck in the small, windowless room.

"Okay," I respond to Elder Steven's lying admission. I know Cain would've asked about me.

I just know.

There's a knock on the door, and Elder Steven steps forward. Elder William enters the room, looks me up and down, then turns to Elder Steven. "Is she ready?"

"Nearly."

"How long before she's reprogrammed?"

Reprogrammed?

"She's still got fight in her. I can see it. She doesn't totally believe everything. I always liked the fire she had, but this may be my best opportunity to break everything out of her."

Why are they talking about me like I'm not here?

Because that's what they do. That's what they've always done. Girls are nothing to them. They talk about us like we're beneath them. Like we're here only for them.

This gets my mind turning. Now I have more questions, questions I'm sure they won't answer. I bite my tongue, wanting to scream at them, but I'm acutely aware I'm stuck in here and won't get out until they think they've broken me. Is that what reprogramming means?

"How much longer? We can't keep her in here for too long. The boy's asking questions."

Boy?

"A few more days should have her completely reset."

Days?

I haven't heard those words before. What are they? I want to ask. But I won't. Instead, I stare at the floor, and not react as they're talking. "You've done an excellent job with her, Steven. At first I wasn't too keen on using water-boarding, but it seems to have worked in your favor."

I want to look up, and yell at them. But if I want to get out of here, I have to keep quiet.

I hear the door creaking shut, before it closes, Elder William laughs. "This is enough to drive anyone insane." I notice he lifts his hand and points upward toward the ceiling.

"It's getting through to her though." Elder William laughs again, then the door closes. "Now, where were we?" Elder Steven asks me.

I shrug without thinking, internally scolding myself. I shouldn't have done that. "I'm hungry. Please, may I have some food?" I ask attempting to be what I think they want.

My body is weak, but my brain is sharp. Although I know I'm hungry, I'm still listening intently to every word spoken, especially when they talk about me like I'm not here. I'm figuring out you can learn a lot when you listen. I might not be able to read, but I can certainly pick up on words they say. It's not so much the word, but the tone. When Elder William said 'the boy,' the way he said it with complete disgust, I'm assuming 'the boy' indicates someone. And the only someone

I'm close with, is Cain. I've never known Cain as 'the boy' only a man. But, it has to be him. He has to have asked about me.

I'll be devastated if he hasn't asked for me, but I'm confident he has.

"I'll bring you food." My stomach grumbles as if it knows Elder Steven is talking to it. "When I think you're ready," he adds with a smirk.

Usually, I'd tell him how horrible he is. But, this is exactly what he wants. To hear me say something so then he can keep me longer in the windowless room. "Of course," I say. "When you believe, I deserve it." I hate saying the words out loud, of even thinking them to begin with.

"Good girl," he proudly says, walks over to me, and pats me on the head. This isn't something he'd usually do. Girls aren't to be touched, unless we're being disciplined.

It feels wrong though. Almost, like he's making fun of me or something.

"After this little stunt of yours, I think I'll talk to William about moving our wedding date up. I'm sure I'll be able to convince him."

The hair on the back of my neck stands. My stomach churns with revulsion. "Who will I marry?" He's made no secret, it'll be him. But I need to hear him say it.

"I'll be your husband, Luna. I'll be the one who'll be in bed with you every night. And soon, you'll bear my child. And we'll start all over again, and again, *and again.*" He's talking as if he's proud, and excited. He rubs at the bulge in front of his pants, then lets out a small cough.

The repulsion I feel fuels my need to get out of here. To finally leave this behind. I'll take Cain with me. He needs to know everything I know. And we need to leave, together.

I just have to make it out of this windowless room alive.

CHAPTER FIFTEEN

"HOW ARE YOU today, Luna?"

Elder William doesn't want to know the real answer. Elder Steven doesn't care, or he wouldn't keep me in here. Elder William's just as bad. He allows Elder Steven to treat me like this, so, why would he care?

"I'm good today, Elder William," I say with false sweetness in my voice.

"You're looking better. The bruising has gone down."

"We are your family. Beyond the wall is death. Beyond the wall is evil. You will die if you leave. Only we can protect you," the female voice hasn't stopped chanting. It's enough to send a person over the edge, but I have the few memories of the outside I keep hold of. They have gotten me through this. They've made me stronger, and smarter.

Not smarter as in I can read, but as soon as I get out of here, I'm going to learn how to do that. But smarter in a way that I know there's so much more than what they've been telling us. And I want to understand everything we haven't been allowed to learn in here.

I know there's more beyond the wall. I've seen it with my own eyes. That small part can't be all of it, *it can't be.*

"I feel better," I say as I push off the cold floor and back up until I feel the cool of the wall against my clothed back.

"I think it might be a good idea to bring you out. But, I need to make sure you're not a threat to the rest of our family."

I narrow my eyes and tilt my head to the side. "A threat?"

"Yes, you see…" Elder William stops talking and walks around to stand opposite me. "If you want to tell anyone about what you saw beyond the wall, I'll be forced to do something I don't want to."

Shaking my head vigorously at him, I add in a small voice, "I won't say anything."

"Well, Luna. If you do, I'll be forced to hurt…"

"I know, me. I know what waits for me and I can promise you, I won't say a word. I don't want to be back here. Or to…" The memory of Elder Steven's happy face as he struck me over and over again, floods my memory. I remember every blow of his hands as they connected with my face and body.

"No, not you."

I look up at him, the vision of Elder Steven dunking my head in the water vanishes. His evil eyes disappear. The smirk of satisfaction he had is now gone. "What do you mean?"

"I won't hurt you. Not at all. I couldn't do that to you." He walks over to me, grabs my chin roughly in his hand, softly stroking my cheek with his thumb. This is similar to something Elder Steven did to me, just before he hit me. I'm not fooled by his gentleness. "I'll bring Cain in here, tie him up, make you watch while we torture him. You were water-boarded, I may use boiling water on him. What do you think, Luna? Do you think you'd like to watch that?"

Dunking his head in boiling water? Who would do something so cruel?

My mouth is open, and my brows are drawn together. My body is filled with panic and dread. "We are your family. Beyond the wall is death. Beyond the wall is evil. You will die if you leave. Only we can protect you," the female voice chants.

They call themselves family, I call them evil. "Why would you do that?" I ask, horrified, and afraid.

"I'm letting you know what the consequences are if you talk about anything."

"I wouldn't." Not now, not knowing what

Elder William is prepared to do to Cain.

"So, we're clear then. If you talk, we'll have to hurt Cain. And just to give you an extra incentive, if you talk, we'll also hurt Abigail, Sister Julie and Sister Polly."

"Why would you do that?" I ask in a small whisper. I bring my hand to my mouth, even more terrified of saying anything now their safety is in my hands.

"I've developed a safe world here. And if you start telling people there's more outside, then I'll make everyone you love bleed, all while you're watching. I'm not going to have a fifteen-year-old bitch ruin everything I've worked for."

"A fifteen-year-old bitch? What's a bitch?"

The look on his face, morphs very quickly from calm to rage. His cheeks flush, and his eyes widen. "Are you listening to anything I've told you?" he screams in my face.

I'm no longer frightened by anything he's said. The words are said to control me, put fear into me. They're not my family, because although I have no idea what family should be like, I know unequivocally, family wouldn't be so cruel. "I've heard everything you've said," I finally respond with ice in my voice. I have to put on a brave exterior for them. Though inside the feelings I have range from anger to sadness mixed with a slight tinge of fear too. I have to be very careful of what I say, and who I say it too.

"Then I see no use in keeping you in here any longer." I nod my head, and heed his warning. I take it seriously. "I'll let Elder Steven know you're to come out." I don't respond. I don't dare say a word. "Maybe you can reflect on what I said, let it sink in how serious I am."

I laugh lifelessly. *Let it sink in,* he says. "I understand," I say with a frustrated sigh. "I talk, you hurt Cain."

"Precisely, my child."

Rolling my eyes, I shake my head. "Your child?" I chuckle again. Then I say the words I've heard over and over again. "We are your family. Beyond the wall is death. Beyond the wall is evil. You will die if you leave. Only we can protect you." My tone is harsh, and angry. "Only we can protect you," I say again. "Only *we* can protect you." I spit the word 'we' at him. "I feel so incredibly protected here."

Elder William smirks at me. "I'm glad we have a clear understanding then. Until I see you on the outside, Luna."

Outside. What a word. I'll be more confined 'outside' than I am here. At least in here, I know they're watching me, playing the same recording over and over again. Beyond these walls, I have all the room I could want to move around in, but I'm still held against my choice. How much freedom do I really have?

None.

He closes the door.

The voice keeps playing.

I sit on the floor, lower my head, close my eyes, and remember the images of beyond the wall.

I can't wait to get back out there again, but I know it won't be anywhere near as easy to leave again. Without realizing it, I fall asleep.

"Is this what you wanted to happen?" I look up, and see everyone staring at me. My wrists are tied behind me, at the whipping pole.

"I'm sorry, I won't do it again," I scream.

Elder Steven laughs. "We gave you the opportunity to say nothing. We warned you about what was going to happen."

I desperately seek Cain's eyes to help calm me, but he's nowhere. I can't see him anywhere. "Where's Cain?" I yell.

"Cain's dead, because of you."

"NO!" I scream and cry.

"You brought pain to Abigail. You brought death to Cain." Everyone murmurs. "Should we continue to allow Luna to bring you all pain and death?" Elder Steven calls to everyone.

"No," everyone choruses together.

"Should we allow Luna to bring disruption to our community any longer?"

"No!" everyone says, this time with more anger in their reply.

"Should we allow Luna to rule us here?"

"NO!" everyone shouts, louder again. They close in on me, coming closer and closer.

"Luna spreads lies about what's beyond the wall. She would have you believe there's no death, or illness. She'll try to convince you how there's good outside the wall. If you're sick of her lies, of her manipulation, then tell her. Tell her now!" He shouts so loud, everyone is feeding off his energy.

"We hate you, Luna."

"Stop your lies."

"Kill her!"

So many things are being yelled at me, and even though I can hear them individually, I don't know who's saying what.

"Today, your reign of terror ends," Elder Steven says. "Everyone, go find a rock, and bring it back here. Today, we're going to have a stoning of this witch. Stone the witch, and the lies end with her."

Everyone runs off, picking up stones and rocks. Even the younglings are bringing back rocks they can carry.

"No! Stop, can't you see what they're doing? They're filling your heads with lies. They want you to kill me, so you never know what's on the outside. There's more than they're telling us. I saw it, I saw it with my own eyes."

"Kill the witch."

"Kill the liar."

"Kill her."

My heart is racing, and I'm trying desperately to break the ties around my wrists. I'm trying, but they won't give.

Elder Steven walks over to me. The commotion behind him is like nothing I've ever experienced. Everyone is so angry, waiting for him to give them permission to hurt me.

"All you had to do was keep your mouth shut," he whispers in my ear.

"But I never said anything. Why are you doing this?"

"Because, Luna. It's all your fault."

"I never said a word. Why… why?" I cry as I look up at him.

"It's all your fault." He steps backward while smiling at me. "She's all yours," he says to everyone.

The first stone hits me in the head, and I scream in pain. The rest come at me so fast, I barely have enough time to close my eyes.

Startling awake, I sit up and gasp. "What was that?" Running my hand over my forehead, I wipe at the sweat gathering. Shaking my head, I try to dislodge the image of the crowd closing in and so angry at me.

I get to my feet and begin to pace. My heart is racing, and I try to convince myself that it was only a dream. It may have been a dream, but I'm now positive. The Elders are capable of stoning me to death, and much *much* more.

CHAPTER SIXTEEN

"Remember what we talked about," Elder Steven says as he steps back from the door.

"I know," I reply.

"You talk, we'll hurt everyone but you. And you will be made to watch."

"I know." Sickness fills my stomach. I hate how they keep telling me this. *I know.*

"The story is, you fell sick and you were isolated so you wouldn't make everyone else sick," he says proudly. I have to doubt everything I've ever heard when he can easily lie to everyone.

"So, I've been sick. What type of sick was I?" I question.

"No one will ask," he confidently replies. "And if someone does, just say it was something with a big name that you can't recall." I nod my head. Anger still bubbling away inside me. "And about our wedding," he says as he walks me through a dimly lit, short hallway until we're at another door. "It'll be happening shortly. You'll be of age soon, but our wedding will be happening before that."

Great. I also know it's of no use to argue. It's not going to get me anywhere, except back in the windowless room with the cold floor. "Okay," I barely manage through my tight jaw.

The door opens, and we're in Elder Steven's room. I've wondered where this door leads, and now I know. I look over to his bed, and the sun coming in from the window nearly blinds me. I look away and shelter my eyes. "It's so bright," I say.

"Just sit, and wait until your eyes adjust." He points to the side of his bed, but revulsion overtakes me. There's no way I want to be anywhere near his bed. Not now, not ever.

"I'm fine," I say as I continue to blink and try to adjust to the sunlight.

He laughs, and makes a sound as if to say, *'Sure, you're fine.'*

I continue until we're both outside his room. He pulls the door closed behind me. I want to run to find Cain, and tell him about everything, but I've also been made aware of the consequences of my actions *if* I do that.

"Luna!" I hear Cain's voice from somewhere behind me.

Turning, I blink, my eyes finally adjusting to the

brightness. Cain runs toward me, and stops short of hugging me when he sees the angry scowl Elder Steven is giving him. It's not hard to miss. Elder Steven is only a heartbeat away from being super angry. "Why are you like this?" I ask under my breath.

"I don't like the way he looks at you."

"We are your family. Beyond the wall is death. Beyond the wall is evil. You will die if you leave. Only we can protect you," I repeat to him in a clipped tone.

Elder Steven glares at me sideways. "Cain," he says. He turns and walks away.

Cain stares after Elder Steven, and smiles at me. "Where have you been?"

I turn to look over my shoulder, and can see Elder Steven hovering, listening. "I got sick. Really sick. They had to isolate me from everyone because they didn't know if what I had, could be passed on." The lie rolls off my tongue like I've been practicing it.

"What did you have?" He starts walking backward, and gestures with his head toward the wall, our spot.

"I'm not sure what I had. The Elders told me, but I can't remember. It was a long word." I smile, trying to convince Cain.

Silently we walk to the wall. When we get to a tree, Cain sits, and pats the grass beside him. I sit, but further away. "Are you okay?"

"I'm okay." I offer a smile.

Cain watches me, then squints his eyes at me. He shakes his head. "I don't think so."

"Why?"

He leans forward, and stares at my face. "What happened to your face, Luna?"

"Nothing, why?" I shield my eyes against the sunlight, knowing exactly what he's seeing.

"You have bruising around your eyes and mouth."

"I fell," I automatically respond. More lying, something I never thought I'd do. Especially to Cain.

"Oh," he says and sits back. "What happened?"

I move my hands down, and shuffle back a bit more. "I got sick, and I fell. Hit my face on the ground." I avoid his eyes. I hate lying to him. But the consequences are too big to ignore. I tell Cain, and they'll hurt him, and others too.

"I'm glad the Elders looked after you." He smiles.

Looked after me. What a joke. They didn't look after me, they hurt me because they think I'm a threat. They called me a bitch. I'm still not sure what a bitch is, but I'm also smart enough to know, it's not something nice. "They looked after me, alright." I add an eye roll, but quickly pull back when I realize Cain's watching me.

"Tell me what happened?"

Where do I start? I got out from digging a hole under a wire fence, saw some of the outside world, somehow ended up back in here, was beaten, had my head dunked and held under water, and you were threatened. "I felt sick, fell, and ended up in a room, in isolation." I swallow back the lies. "I had to stay until I was better."

"But you were gone for many days."

"I know. The Elders had to make sure it was safe for me to come out, and not make everyone sick."

"But they wouldn't tell me anything about you."

"You asked?"

"I asked all of the Elders. None of them said where you were or what was happening. I was worried, Luna, so, worried. I'm just glad you're back." He sneaks his hand out, hoping to touch my fingers. I move back even more. He's not going to get hurt because of me. "Luna?" he questions. His voice is laced with hurt. But he has no idea of the pain they can bring him. The pain *I* can bring him.

"I was sick," I say in a dead pan voice. Though, I'm trying my hardest to hold in the tears. Cain asked about me, and that fills my heart with love for him. But it also rips it apart too. Because now, I have to distance myself from him. I can't risk what they're capable of doing to him. *I can't.*

"I don't understand why they wouldn't tell me anything." He scrubs his hand over his chin.

Standing, I walk away from him as a tear rolls down my cheek. Discreetly, I wipe it away. I don't say anything, I don't trust my voice to remain steady. But I make a decision to not be Cain's friend anymore. I have to, because it'll kill me if *I* kill *him*.

I have to protect him.

"Why couldn't they tell me you were sick? I would've come to sit with you," he pushes.

It's my opportunity to start friction between us. To make him hate me, so he doesn't get hurt. I pull my shoulders back, lift my head and take a deep breath. Turning, I give him a sweet smile. The words I'm about to say, aren't words I'd usually speak. "Because I told them I didn't want you to know."

"Why?" He too stands, and walks toward me.

"Because, Cain. You don't need to know." The words come out harsher than I want them to.

Cain squints at me. "What?" His face is questioning, exactly like his reply.

I need this to hurt him. As much as I can. For his safety. "Because, Cain, you're not worth my effort. I realized while I was sick and Elder Steven was taking care of me, I need to respect him now I'm going to be his bride." The words cut like a freshly sharpened pair of scissors. "And, I told them not to let you know *if* you asked for me." Tears well in my eyes, but I hold it together. I have to.

"If?" Cain steps back, his hand flying to his heart, as if I've speared him and he's wounded. "*If?*" he asks again. "*If,* Luna? I was so worried, I searched for you, in case you went into the diseased trees. I risked my life, and went into the trees to find you. I came back when Elder William saw me walking into the trees, and came after me. He told me you'd taken ill, and would let me see you when you were better. But he didn't say anything again. I was worried, Luna. So worried, I could barely sleep. Don't you dare say *if.*"

I want to tell him. To grab his hand, run through the trees until we find the wire, and crawl under it. I want to tell him everything. Instead, I bite my tongue. Forbidden to breathe a word of what really happened. His safety is all I want. I don't care what they do to me, but they've told me, they'll hurt Cain and make me watch.

I step back from him, lift my chin higher. "I'd rather serve the Elders in the dining room than continue talking to you, Cain."

"But…" He shakes his head. "You hate serving them."

I narrow my lips, holding onto my feelings as much as I can. "Exactly," I spit toward him.

"I'm…" Cain looks down at my feet, *hurt.* Does he actually believe me? Please no, please yes. I'm so conflicted. I want him safe, but I don't want him to hate me. But hating me means he *will* remain safe.

"Your problem is this." I hate this person the Elders are making me into. "Your problem, is you're not smart enough to think for yourself. You and I were friends, because I was smarter than you."

"Were friends? Luna, we were more than friends. I love you."

My heart shatters. "I don't love you." More lies. I walk past him, and don't look over my shoulder at him. I walk with my head held high, but with tears streaming down my cheeks. This is beyond heart-breaking. It's shattering everything inside of me. It's like a piece of me has died. I love Cain. I love him so much, I'm willing to make him hate me for being horrible, in order to save him.

I approach the main house, and notice Elder Steven standing by the door. "Good chat?" he asks.

I look up at him, and he laughs at me when he sees my tears. "I did what I had to, to keep him safe. Don't worry, I'm all alone now."

He smirks at me. "Just the way I like my brides."

I glare at him. There's nothing nice about him. Not one thing. He's exactly what they warn us of. He is evil. He is diseased. Inside the wall is death. I will die if I stay here.

I'd rather die as I try to leave, then live and be stuck here.

CHAPTER SEVENTEEN

THE SUN HAS risen and set many times, and I've yet to speak with Cain. It's safest this way. He can't get hurt because of me. Actually, I've separated myself from everyone. I don't want to talk with or be nice to anyone. I grumble my answers, if I'm asked a question. I keep my head down, and try not to make eye contact with anyone at all.

It's been miserable. *I've* been miserable.

But it's the only way I know to keep everyone safe around me. The Elders, especially Elder Steven, have been watching me. I can feel his beady eyes on me, all the time, wherever I go. He appears where I am, watching me, trying to talk to me. I ignore him and walk away. And I don't even care that he can whip me. Truth be told, the only thing I care about is keeping everyone safe, and trying to figure out a way to leave here.

Sister Rachel approaches me as I clean the kitchen, snapping me out of my anger toward

Elder Steven. "Luna, can we talk?" she asks.

I don't look up, but her sweet voice has a tinge of desperation to it. "I'm busy," I snap at her. If she wants to get close to me, I have to stop it now.

Sister Rachel is only slightly older than me. She was of age recently, and married Elder Jacob. Elder Jacob is fairly quiet, he's one of the newest Elders to join God's Haven. He doesn't speak like Elder Steven, and he doesn't have many wives. He only has Sister Rachel. He's different than all the other Elders. He comes into the dining room, eats, and never joins in conversation with the others.

Sister Rachel seems different since she married Elder Jacob. She's quiet by nature too, but she seems a bit more reserved than she's ever been.

"Please," she says in a slightly more urgent voice.

Sister Rachel has always been kind to me. And I really shouldn't be horrible to her, but I can't risk her getting close to me either. I take a deep breath, look down at the floor remaining, then lift my head and smile at her. "Of course," I reply.

"Come, sit with me." She lifts her hand and offers it to me so she can help pull me up. Touching among the girls isn't forbidden, not like it is between the men and the girls. But it's not encouraged either.

Taking her hand in mine, I hoist myself up, and walk behind her. She walks to the front, and sits on the steps outside the door. "Elder Jacob has instructed me to speak with you," she says.

"What about?" My curiosity is high.

"About you wedding Elder Steven."

I look away to roll my eyes, not wanting her to see my disgust for him. "What about it?" I ask trying to hide my revulsion.

"Becoming a bride is a rite of passage," she says, obviously detecting the distaste in my words.

I turn back to her, and plaster a fake smile on my face. "Of course." I smile larger. I thought Sister Rachel would be different; clearly, I was mistaken.

But then again, all we've been fed is lies. Lies about everything on the outside. Why would she think any different?

"I'm sorry," I say, trying to calm my irritation with her.

She smiles and I know, she believes me. "You'll be a bride soon." I nod, and fake smile again. "Elder Jacob told me to talk to you, so you know what to expect."

Doing? I know. The Elder will put his penis inside my vagina. It's been explained to me. "Are you talking about sex?" I ask.

"You know about sex?" She brings her hand up to cover her mouth, shocked. "How do you know?"

"One of the Sisters told me."

"Who? Who told you?"

"Um…" I can't say, because she'll get in trouble. "I don't remember." *Please believe me.* I really don't want to see anyone get in trouble. I've been working so hard to isolate myself, that small error now makes me angry with myself.

Her eyes carefully watch my features, scrutinizing me. I've felt those judging eyes with Elder Steven. "Well," she starts. "The vows of a bride to her Elder are sacred."

"And what about the vows of the Elder to his bride?"

She laughs. "They don't take a vow to us. We are here for them. To please them, to look after them, to be everything they want us to be, *for them.*" I've only seen a glimpse to the outside world, but something inside me says, we are not alive only for the Elders. "Our vows to our Elder are done in secret."

"Why?" Now, I'm genuinely curious about what we're supposed to do. Not because I'm interested, more like, because I know whatever has been created is to benefit only the Elders.

"It's an honor, Luna. This tone is making me think you won't be honored when Elder Steven takes you as his."

I bite on my tongue. I want to tell her that I don't want to be Elder Steven's, or anyone else's bride. But, I can't. Not now that I know there's more to the Elders. "I'm sorry. I'm still not feeling well." I run my hand across my stomach, in hope of her believing me. "Please, continue." Trying with everything I have in me, I focus on her and try to externally show my enthusiasm.

"The vows are simple. Elder William will take you into a room, and he will prepare you." I scrunch my nose. "Not like that. That'll be up to Elder Steven if he allows another Elder to have access to your body." Bile rises to the back of my throat. "Being wanted by the Elders is almost as big an honor as marrying an Elder."

Don't say anything, Luna. Keep your mouth shut. Smile, and nod. Smile and nod.

"Of course," I say though really there's no way I want any of them touching me. Elder Steven least of all.

"Elder William will take you into a room. He'll prepare you by removing your clothing."

"Removing my clothes?" I look down to the dress I wear, and cringe. "All of it?"

"Yes, you'll be before him, naked."

"Naked?" I nearly shriek. "He'll see my private areas? My breasts, my vagina?"

She laughs. "Of course, he must prepare you for your vows."

"But I have to be naked to speak my vows?"

She laughs again, a big hearty laugh. "You don't speak, Luna. That's part of our vows. You say nothing. You listen to instruction from Elder William, and do what he tells you."

I swallow the spit gathering in my mouth. This

is becoming more disturbing as the conversation continues. "Are you sure?"

"This is how we women have been wed since before the wall. This is how it was done when there was an outside that wasn't filled with death and disease."

How does she know? Has she seen it for herself? Of course not. We're told what *they* want us to know. "This is the way of the bride?" I ask more to myself than her.

"Yes. These will be your vows. Elder William will inspect you, check you over to make sure you're ready for Elder Steven. He will say some words which are sacred, so I cannot repeat them to you. He'll lead you to the bed, lay you down, open your legs, and wait for Elder Steven to enter the room. Once Elder Steven enters, he'll disrobe, climb on the bed and tell you his vows."

"Are they sacred too?"

"No, those are beautiful. All of us wives hear the most beautiful words."

"Which are?"

"He will climb between your open legs, he'll push inside you and whisper, 'You belong to me.' Once those words are spoken, your heart will be his forever."

Really? That's it? There's nothing nice or sweet about that. He'll push inside me and whisper I'm his? "That's it?" I ask.

"What do you mean?" I look over to her, to see

how her gaze is far away, as if she's remembering her time with Elder Jacob. "It's beautiful."

"It doesn't sound beautiful to me. More like ownership," I challenge, unfortunately too loud.

Sister Rachel whips her head around, her eyes filled with anger, her jaw hard with fury. "We belong to them. You should feel honored you're wanted, not so selfish, Luna. They look after us, and we serve them."

Truthfully, I'm not even shocked by her irritation. This is what we've been taught, this is how we've been brought up. To believe the Elders are our protectors. But I've seen another side to them, and they're not what they've led us to believe they are.

"I'm sorry," I apologize. I don't want her to go and tell any of the Elders about how resistant I am. "You are my family. Beyond the wall is death. Beyond the wall is evil. Only the Elders can protect us," I say, hearing the female voice in my head. "But, I do have a question."

Sister Rachel's face softens, and she smiles. "What is it?"

"Does Elder William stay in the room while the Elder says his vows?"

"Of course. He has to check."

"Check for what?"

"Check for blood." I tilt my head to the side, not understanding what she's talking about. Sister Rachel giggles and runs her hand over my back in slow gentle circles. It's the closest thing to a hug I've gotten from a Sister in a long time. "When he pushes inside you, you bleed."

"Like when I menstruate?"

"Different. It hurts. It's uncomfortable, but it's the ultimate sacrifice a girl makes. She must bleed for her Elder."

"I still don't understand."

"The Elder will push his penis inside you. And it does something to your vagina. You'll bleed."

"What if I don't?"

"That's just silly talk. Of course, you will."

Now I'm really anxious about it, although, I hope to find myself out of here long before that happens. I don't want Elder Steven anywhere near me, let alone, inside me. "But, what if I don't?" I ask again.

She shrugs and smiles. "I can't answer that. I bled," she says proudly.

"Does Elder William leave once he sees the blood?"

"What? No, he stays to make sure the Elder finishes, and leaves you full of seed to bear his child." Although she's not telling me specifically what she means, just those words are enough for me to throw up in my mouth. "But, sometimes it takes many attempts to put a baby in a girl's body." She rubs at her stomach and smiles. "I'm with child," she says with a huge smile.

I'm happy for her, if that's what she wants. But I don't want that. Not with Elder Steven. I want to see the outside world first, experience everything I can before I'm with child. I know it sounds selfish, but there's more than what we have in here.

"And then does Elder William leave after?"

She laughs again. "Yes, he doesn't come back in again. Well, not unless he requests you for his pleasure."

Yuck. "Does that happen often?" *Please say no.*

"The Elders can request you any time they want, however it's up to the Elder you belong to if they share you with the others. It's a great honor to be wanted by many."

"Have you been requested by many?" I'm thoroughly repulsed by the notion, but also absolutely intrigued. Something seems quite unhealthy about being requested and going to whichever Elder wants you for their pleasure, without having any say in it.

She tilts her head down, her cheeks pinking with embarrassment. She's going to tell me a lot of the Elders have requested, or only some. "I'm not as wanted as some other brides." She smiles, and I can see the smile is meant to deflect from her sadness. She wants them to want her? No thank you. I'd rather they don't want me. "But don't worry, I think you're going to be wanted by *all* the Elders." Her tone tells me she's genuinely happy for me, and not jealous.

"Great." I cringe. Exactly what I don't want.

"It's an honor, Luna. I've heard them talking, and Elder Steven is quite protective of you. He's giving the other Elders conditions on what they're allowed to do to you."

"What about what I want?"

"You're so silly." She laughs again. Why does she find this funny? It's a serious question. "We want what our Elder wants for us."

No, no I don't. I don't want what *my* Elder wants. I don't even want to be owned by an Elder. There's nothing appealing about this to me. Nothing, not one little bit. No use in speaking the words in my head. "Of course, we do." *No, I don't.*

Sister Rachel stands, straightens her dress and smiles. "My work here is done. You'll be taking your vows before the next full moon. I'm so happy for you, Luna. You'll finally be one of the wives."

I don't reply. I have nothing nice to say.

"But, between you and me, I've heard Momma Edith talking to Momma Kim, and neither of them seem too happy with you."

"Why?"

"As you know, they're Elder Steven's wives, and they don't like new brides being introduced."

"But Elder Steven has more wives than Momma Edith and Momma Kim."

"Yes, but Elder Steven has been talking about

you and only you. I think they feel left out. And when you become his bride, it means they'll be pushed aside. I know Elder Steven often shares a bed with them together, and now there won't be enough room for them with you there."

A shudder rips through me, but at least I don't have to work at making them hate me. They already do, without me doing anything. I smile and think quickly what to say, because Sister Rachel's eyes are watching me, waiting for a reply. "I hope we can all be close."

"This has been nice, Luna. I'm so happy you'll be joining us soon. And I really hope, you'll be with child the day you become Elder Steven's."

I'm hoping I'm out of here before the day I become Elder Steven's. Because my fear is once I'm his, I'll never get out alive.

CHAPTER EIGHTEEN

"CURFEW IS AT sunset," Elder William announces to everyone once we've been summoned to the common area centered around the whipping post. "And it will be strictly enforced."

I look around, and stare at everyone's faces. Most of the girls gaze at Elder William like he's the sun. I haven't really noticed this before, the intent and captivating way they look at him. It's almost like he's speaking words filled with beauty and laced with harmony. They're completely mesmerized by it. All I hear is lies.

"Furthermore, you may not know, but soon we'll be having a wedding." The girls all coo and giggle. I feel sick to my stomach because I know what Elder William is going to say. "With the next full moon, Elder Steven will be taking Luna as his bride."

Some of the girls turn to look, scowling quite obviously toward me. I want to scream at them, *you can have him,* but of course, I won't. Other girls whisper something to each other, and they giggle. I turn away, not wanting to see, or hear anything they do. I don't want this for myself. They can take my place.

As I turn away, I catch a glimpse of Abigail, who's standing at the back and by herself. She has tears rolling down her cheeks. She upsets me most. Not because she's crying, but because she's always been so desperate to have the attention of the Elders, and she's never received it. I wish I could switch places with her, for her to have their attention, and for them to leave me alone. Although the image of her broken, still scars me and I wouldn't want that for anybody.

"Luna, Abigail, and Ava, you're all needed in the dining room for dinner."

Abigail notices me looking at her, lifts her chin, then nods to Elder William. As if she has a choice. If you're a girl, you don't get a choice in anything. *Because it's our duty.* The Elders protect us, and we serve them. *Lies, lies and more lies.*

I turn off to the rest of what Elder William says, it's like he's nothing more than noise. I can't stand the lies any longer.

Everyone begins walking away, which tells me we can leave and the Elders have finished addressing us.

I walk over to the main kitchen, where some of my sisters are back to preparing dinner for the

Elders.

Abigail pushes past me, making me stumble forward. "Seems like some of us are extremely popular with the Elders. I don't know why." She turns, stares at me, and lets her eyes roam over my body. "It's not like you're pretty or anything."

I bite on the inside of my cheek, stopping myself from saying anything to her. If she hates me, then that means she's not close to me. Which means, they won't hurt her *because* of me.

"Leave her alone, Abigail," Ava says as she walks in behind me.

"It's okay," I reply.

"No, it's not. Abigail's being nasty."

"It's alright," I say again, as I pick up some plates and start walking them toward the dining room.

I feel it before I see it. Someone grabs my hair, and throws themselves on top of me. There's a lot of yelling and screaming, and things being said. "It's because of you I'll never get picked by an Elder." The plates going flying out of my hands as I fall forward, my face breaking my fall.

Blood spurts out of my nose, as I feel someone grab my hair again, and try to smash my face into the floor. I don't need to guess who it is, I know. *It's Abigail.* The venom in her voice is all I need to hear to know it's her.

I try to protect my head, but she manages to hit me once across the back of my head before I feel her being pulled off me. "Enough, Abigail," Elder Steven's voice is unmistakable. It's deep and incredibly controlled.

"She started it!" Abigail yells as she points toward me.

"Yes, I did," I say, wanting to take the brunt of whatever is going to happen to Abigail. She's been hurt enough because of me, I can't have her broken again.

"No, Elder Steven, it wasn't Luna, she was walking away when Abigail threw herself on her, and started hitting her," Ava says.

No Ava, what are you doing? "I started it," I say again, trying to silence Ava with just a look.

"No, she didn't do anything," Ava says again, trying to defend me. If only she knew the consequences, but of course, she doesn't.

Ava, please, stop. "I did it," I challenge again, and look at Ava, trying desperately to make her understand what I'm attempting to do.

"Luna, a word." Elder Steven releases Abigail's arm, and walks away from them, expecting me to follow. When he stops, he looks behind me to make sure we're not within listening distance of the others. "Either you're lying or Ava is lying. If Ava is lying, she'll be publically whipped. If you're lying, then you'll be publically whipped. Choose."

"I'm lying," I say too quickly. I refuse to let another girl take a punishment because of me.

"Abigail started it?" It's not a question, more a statement. I nod my head and look down to the ground. "She'll be dealt with. Go to the whipping post." I begin to walk away, and he says in a low voice, "I'm looking forward to this."

A tear falls from my eye. I'm not afraid of the whipping, but I hate how Elder Steven has the power to do so. But I walk to the whipping post, and wrap my arms around it. Everyone comes to the center to watch. They all know from me wrapping my arms around the whipping post what's about to happen.

"Luna, what happened?" Cain asks from beside me. I don't want to look at him, I don't want to see the worry in his eyes.

"Please, don't watch," I whisper to him, hopeful he'll walk away and not have to witness what I'm about to go through.

"What happened?" he asks again.

"I lied. I said something happened that didn't, and now I'm being punished. Please, Cain, I won't make it through if I know you're watching. Please, please, just leave," I beg him to listen to me. I know girls don't give orders, but I'm hoping this time, he listens.

"I thought we weren't friends any more, Luna." His words tear at my heart. More than the whip will tear at my back. "I thought you didn't love me anymore."

I want to tell him. Really want to open my

mouth and tell him everything I know. From behind Cain, I see Elder Steven walking toward me. In his hand, is his belt. He's holding it from the end without the buckle. He smiles at me. He really is going to enjoy this.

"I don't," I whisper to Cain. "I don't love you anymore. I'll be Elder Steven's soon, and I won't ever love you again."

I want to look away from Cain, but I can't. I see the hurt in his eyes. His heart is breaking all over again too. Mine has already been ripped into many parts, none of them working properly. The Elders have destroyed me. They've ruined me, and they don't care. Elder Steven will take his sick enjoyment from me any way he can. Be it whipping, or in his bed as his bride.

Cain backs away from me. His face tells me exactly how much I'm hurting him. I hate myself for doing this.

Elder Steven sees the look on my face, and I can only imagine what he's seeing. A girl who's broken. A girl who's in so much pain, because she's forced to send the only good thing in God's Haven away.

"Cain." Elder Steven stops Cain from leaving.

"Yes." Cain looks over his shoulder to me, then back to Elder Steven.

A smirk reaches Elder Steven's mouth. The same grin I saw when he was beating me in the windowless room. The same satisfaction crossing his face. "It's time you stepped up."

Fear creeps into my body. Please, no, don't ask him to do what I think you're going to.

"What can I help with, Elder Steven?" Cain asks eagerly.

Please… no.

Silently, Elder Steven extends his hand, giving Cain the belt.

"NO!" I yell. No, please, don't let this happen. "Please, no, not Cain. You do it, Elder Steven. I deserve this from you." Crying, I beg Elder Steven to not do this. I can't. I can't deal with it. If Cain's the one holding the belt, it'll destroy me. "Please," I beg.

Elder Steven doesn't flinch as he holds his hand out further to Cain.

"Please," I whisper. Tears stream down my cheeks. My eyes are so blurry from crying, that I can barely make out Elder Steven and Cain.

"I'll do it," I hear from behind me. I don't need to turn to know it's Abigail. "She deserves everything she's going to get."

Elder Steven thrusts the belt in Cain's hand and angrily walks over to Abigail. He grabs her by the upper arm, and pulls her to stand in front of me. "You can watch from here." I don't know why he's doing this. Elder Steven is nasty and cruel, but this is particularly horrible. "Cain, you have a choice. Start your journey to become an Elder, or stay a man and never live up to your full potential."

"I don't want…" Cain looks to me, and sees me crying. "I…" He's confused, and obviously conflicted about what to do.

"Journey to becoming an Elder, or say no to becoming an Elder in front of all your brothers, and the girls," Elder Steven provokes Cain. I hate the power he has. He's trying to intimidate Cain, bully him to do something he clearly doesn't want to do.

"Please," I beg Elder Steven. "Please don't do this."

Elder Steven comes to stand beside me. He leans down, and whispers, "I saw the way you were looking at him, and it sickens me to know you still have feelings for him. I'm going to be the person you belong to, not him. Not now, not ever."

"Please," I beg him. "Don't make him do this."

"I'm not making him do anything. He's choosing." He smiles again, more evil than ever.

"This isn't a choice, not for Cain. Not for me. Please, whip me, hurt me, do whatever you want to me, just don't ask Cain to do this."

"This is what you don't understand, Luna. I *am* doing whatever I want with you. And what I want, is for Cain to hurt as much as you."

"He's done nothing to you, please, stop."

"He loves what belongs to me. And I don't like that, not at all."

"Punish me, please, please." All I'm doing is begging, and all he's doing is loving the sound of me pleading.

"Cain," he says, and for a heartbeat, I hold onto hope that he's going to take the belt from Cain's hand. "Lift your arm back past your head, and bring it down hard."

I look him straight in the eyes, and pull my shoulders back. "You will not break me," I say through a clenched jaw to Elder Steven.

"I know, but I'll destroy him." He's a monster. The monsters they say we should be afraid of. "Cain," he says his name in a low, though strong voice. As if it's a warning.

Turning my head to look at Cain, I smile at him, and nod. "Just do it," I say.

Cain is fighting his own demons, he doesn't want to do this, but he's been backed into a difficult position. He has to. He has no choice. "I can't," he whispers.

"Do it. Don't worry about me, just do it."

"I can't!" Cain yells at me.

"DO IT!" I scream back. The first lash is almost not painful. What hurts most is the satisfaction on Elder Steven's face. I open my eyes and look at Cain. He's got tears falling, and I can see the absolute pain coursing through him.

"Again.

Harder," Elder Steven instructs.

Cain shakes his head at me, and cries some more. "I..."

"Please, just do it," I beg. My own tears are falling, not from the pain I'm feeling, but from the hurt Cain is going through.

He hits me, harder. I let out a pained cry, and I hear Cain let out the same distressed groan. He's hating this as much as I am. And Elder Steven looks too amused. Abigail shares the same joy as Elder Steven, but I don't even care about her. All I care is about what this is doing to Cain.

He hits me again.

I cry out in pain.

He hits.

I cry.

He hits.

I cry.

He hits.

I can't cry anymore.

"Enough," Elder Steven instructs.

Cain drops the belt, and runs away. I fall to my knees, my back blazing with burning pain.

Elder Steven approaches and stands over me. He arches a brow as I look up at him. "Now you know, he'd prefer to be an Elder. He doesn't love you. He probably doesn't even like you."

"I wasn't asking him to choose," I sob.

He smirks, squats beside me and whispers, "But I did."

I don't blame Cain. He was forced to do this, because he doesn't know what I do. "I hate you,"

I say with so much venom running through my voice.

"I know, and this makes it all the more fun for me." Elder Steven stands, and summons Abigail over to me. "Take care of her. Make sure she's looked after. And make sure, you're nice to her."

The more instructions Elder Steven gives Abigail, the more anger flares through her eyes. She doesn't want to take care of me. She doesn't want to be anywhere near me. If I'm being honest, I don't want her anywhere near me, either. Elder Steven leaves, and everyone else follows. Going back to their chores, or whatever it is they were doing. "I don't know why they insist on you even being here," Abigail spits toward me. She walks ahead of me, turns and watches as I struggle to stand and straighten my back. "Hurry up. The last thing I want to do is look after you."

"Abigail, I want you to leave. Don't worry about me."

She laughs and rolls her eyes. "I don't care for you, Luna. You're nothing but a troublemaker. I hate you. I was watching with happiness as Cain whipped you. I hoped he would aim higher, and hit you in the head. Because my life would be better if you weren't here."

I want to tell her everyone's life would be better if I wasn't here. I want to tell her, I'd rather be taking a chance on the outside than be stuck in here where the Elders become more evil with each new sunrise.

CHAPTER NINETEEN

"Where's Abigail? Isn't she supposed to be here on kitchen duty?" Bethany asks as she looks toward the door, expecting Abigail to walk in.

I look too. Wondering where she is. She might hate me, but she never misses her chores. Especially when she's on kitchen or dining duty.

"Abigail won't be here," Momma Edith barks.

I turn to look at her, concerned. "Is Abigail okay?" I ask.

Momma Edith takes a sip from her cup, places it on the small table in the kitchen and folds her arms in front of her chest. Her eyes remain steely, watching me. It's hard for me to move easily, seeing as the wounds on my back are fresh and tender. But I have chores to do. And if I don't do these chores, I'm afraid of what they'll do to the other girls in order to punish me.

Momma Edith's lips draw up in a smile. "She's

fallen suddenly ill, we had to isolate her."

I drop the knife in my hand, and turn to look at Momma Edith completely shocked. My back is screaming in pain, but I know exactly what those words mean. "Abigail," I run out of the kitchen, heading straight toward Elder Steven's room. Knowing there's a door that leads to a secret room in his bedroom. I hit into someone, and don't have a moment to apologize to them. I need to get to Abigail. I need to save her. She won't survive if they do to her, what they did to me.

Although my back is protesting in acute pain, I don't care. I need to help her.

Trying to open his door, I let out a humorless chuckle as I'm met with resistance. "What are you doing?" Elder Steven steps in front of me, causing me to jump in fright.

"Where is she? She won't survive what you did to me." Elder Steven looks around, and it gives me a heartbeat to look around too. Making sure no others are near to hear what I'm saying. I close my eyes, and take a few deep breaths before opening them. "Please, she won't survive." I plead with him.

"She's not in there. And besides, that's a room I use for my pleasure." I'm stuck. What does he mean she's not in there? Where is she? He laughs at my lack of response.

"I don't understand," I say as I step back from his door.

"She's not returning," he replies with zero emotion in his voice.

"She got out?" There's hope in my voice. Something I want for me and I can only hope she got out too. Did she find a way? I really *really* want her out of here.

"Don't be so dumb, Luna. No one gets out, *ever*."

I bring my hand up to scratch an itch on my head. But my brain is attempting to process what he means. "I don't understand," I repeat, slower.

"She's dead."

My heart stutters. Words can't come to me. What does he mean by dead? How? Why? How?…

"She died," he responds to my unasked question. "Slowly, and painfully."

Shaking my head, I fall to my knees. "Why… how?"

"The why is easy. She attacked you. The how is something I'd love to share with you, but I don't think you're ready to hear it yet."

Looking up at him, I'm emotionally blank. "You killed her because she attacked me?"

"Yes," he responds proudly. "And, I'd do it again."

He's a sick, sick man. There's something wrong with him. Suddenly, vomit rapidly makes its way up, and I'm sick in front of him. Bursting into tears, I can't contain my emotions anymore. "You killed her, because of me?" I sob through the words.

"Of course." He's emotionally detached. The way he's casually speaking, it's frustrating because he doesn't care.

"Why?" I don't want to know the answer, so I don't know why I asked.

"Because, I can."

Closing my eyes, I take several deep breaths. And there it is. The answer. It has nothing to do with emotions or feelings, or love. It has to do with control and power. My brain finally understands. Power. He's hungry for it. Is that what this is about? Everything here, is it all about power?

I stop myself from crying, and pick myself up off the floor. Straightening my shoulders, I stand toe to toe with Elder Steven. My back is screaming in pain, but I don't care. He needs to know I'm strong, much stronger than he thinks. Something flashes on his face. Something I haven't seen from him before. But he quickly regains himself, and straightens to his full tall height. I have to tilt my head back to look up at him. But he no longer scares me.

"It has nothing to do with protecting us, does it?"

His brow flinches, and his jaw tightens. I know his secret. I know *their* secret. He doesn't need to respond. I'm quickly working out the answer.

Shaking my head, I step away from him. "This is why girls aren't allowed to learn to read. We pose a threat to what's been built here." I widen my arms, indicating my surroundings. This place I call home.

"No!" he angrily replies. Though I know, just by his response, I'm right, and I'm coming at him face to face. He doesn't like it.

"Then why kill Abigail? Why aren't we allowed to learn? Why must we serve you and you don't serve us?"

He steps forward, rears his hand over his shoulder, and slaps me hard across the face. The force of it sends me to the floor. "Stop asking questions, Luna. I don't want to hurt you." He walks away, angry.

Another lie. He says he doesn't want to hurt me but he does, over and over again.

Standing, I look at his door and feel my heart hurting. He killed Abigail, for no other reason than because of what she did to me. And now, I know. This saddens me more than anything else. Walking back to the kitchen, I begin to chop the vegetables all while thinking of poor Abigail.

"What happened to your face, Luna?" Bethany asks as she stops washing the dirty dishes.

I turn to see Momma Edith smirking at me. She knows. I don't know how, but she does. "I fell," I respond while staring at Momma Edith.

"Let me see if I can put anything on it," Bethany

says as she rushes around me.

"Don't worry about it, it's nothing I can't handle." I keep staring at Momma Edith. "Nothing I'm not used to." Momma Edith's smile begins to fade. "Nothing that won't happen again." She brings her brows together, concerned. "Nothing I won't forget."

Momma Edith stands, and leaves the kitchen.

My arms erupt in little bumps. I'm not frightened by the Elders or Momma Edith anymore. No way. Now, I'm finding my power, my own strength.

"Luna, we have to go outside. Elder William is calling us all," Bethany says.

"Right behind you, Bethany."

We leave the kitchen, and make it out front of the main house where everybody has gathered for the announcements Elder William has for us.

"Men, and girls." Just those words make me roll my eyes. "We have a strict curfew tonight at sundown. Anyone caught out after curfew will be severely punished."

My mind can't let this go. I want to ask how we'll be punished, but, something else is intriguing to me. Why do we have strict curfew? What do they do that they don't want us to see? At sundown tonight, I'll find a way to get out, and see for myself.

"There's also another announcement. Elder Steven will take Luna as his bride in a very short time. There are only a few more days before we have a full moon." I shudder at the thought of our wedding. "Luna is yet to come of age, but we're making an exception. Elder Steven looks forward to introducing a new bride to his wives."

All the girls clap. The men don't care, and the Elders are smiling.

I know I'm going to get out of here the first moment I can. I just need to have the chance to do so.

"Luna, are you excited about your wedding to Elder Steven?" Rose whispers while we're in bed.

"Yes." *No.*

"Elder Steven is the one I hope to marry when I'm of age," Christine says.

"I hope I'm wed to Elder Joshua," Ava says, and giggles.

I hope the vows Elder Steven says to me are over and done with quickly. The thought of him inside me makes me want to vomit. There's nothing appealing about him, or any of them. "You're so lucky, Luna," Christine whispers.

"Quiet now. It's time to sleep," Momma Edith says. We all quiet down, and I wait for her to close the door, so I can sneak out and go see why they want us in bed by sunset.

"Shhh," I call. "I'm tired." I'm not, but I need everyone to get to sleep, so I can sneak out without them seeing me. If they see me, then they may say something, if they say something, either I or they will be punished by the Elders.

I turn over in the bed I'm sharing, waiting patiently for everyone to stop talking, and fall asleep. With me not engaging them in talk about the Elders, they all begin to fall asleep. I listen as their breathing changes from rapid, to soft and even. I wait some more, making sure they're all asleep.

Slowly, I slide out of bed. Making sure I do everything with precision so I don't disturb them. My heart is beating so loudly, I'm bound to wake them. Luckily, they don't stir. I lift myself onto my toes, trying to not put any pressure on the floor so they can't hear the creaks of the wooden floors. I take gentle steps, ensuring quiet. When I reach the door, I place my ear to it, hopeful there's none of the Elders, or the Momma's on the other side. I listen but my hectic heartbeat makes it hard to hear anything but the thumping in my ears. Closing my eyes, I calm myself.

Hearing nothing, I place my hand on the door, and open it as carefully as I can.

I listen. Trying to make any sounds out.

"Where are you going, Luna?" Ava asks in a sleep heavy voice.

"I need to go to the bathroom."

"Okay." Her breathing is heavy as soon as she says the word 'okay.'

Opening the door, I walk out, and I'm met with darkness. Guided by the moon low outside, I walk toward the back door. Looking around, I make sure I can't be seen by the Elders or the Mommas.

I see some of the Elders together, talking and laughing at something. I can't hear what they're saying, because they're too far away. But I'm careful for them not to see me, too. If I'm caught out of bed after curfew, I know I'll be whipped.

Looking up at the moon, I try to follow its shadows and remain unseen.

I bend, even though my back is shouting at me in excruciating pain and I sneak across the field as fast as I can. Making sure to keep an eye on the Elders who haven't noticed me. Maybe they're not expecting us to be out of bed, which is why they're not looking.

I make it to the back, and lie in the short grass, hoping not to be seen.

Looking up at the moon, I watch as it slowly rises higher in the sky. It's quite mesmerizing. Beautiful to watch. Part of it is missing, but as Elder William has said, it'll be full soon, which means I'll become Elder Steven's bride. A shudder tears through me.

Captivated by the beauty of the moon, I barely hear that peculiar rumbling sound again. Being something I think I've heard before, it draws my attention away from the moon. I turn over and see where the sound is coming from. Part of the wall is sliding to the side.

I'm calmer than I was when I initially saw the big hole in the wall. I absorb it, more interested in watching and learning. I'm close enough to see, but far enough to know, the Elders can't see me.

Elder William, Elder Steven and Momma Edith walk toward the opening in the wall. I try to keep low, and behind the shrubs. I listen carefully, trying to hear what they're talking about.

"The girl's going to be a problem. She's piecing it all together," Elder Steven says.

"What have you told her?" Elder William asks.

"He's probably told her all about this place. Fool he is," Momma Edith chuckles.

"Watch yourself, Edith. He's still an Elder," Elder William snaps at her.

"I know. But…"

"You chose this with me. So, you best remember, you're still only a girl."

What does Elder William mean by you chose this with me? I listen more intently. "I'm sorry." Turning to Elder Steven, she says to him, "I'm sorry. I spoke out of turn."

Elder Steven nods to Momma Edith, accepting her apology. "She's putting it all together, and let me tell you if she figures it all out; she has the potential to cause us to crumble. I'm not sure what to do with her."

"We can isolate her again. Play the recording

until they're the only words she knows," Momma Edith offers. I know I'm not smart, like the men, but I also know they must be talking about me.

"That won't break her. She's strong. I've never seen anyone so young have so much fight in them," Elder Steven replies. He lifts his hand and runs it through his hair. I squint, but my eyes have adjusted, and I can see everything, even under the moonlight.

"Get her pregnant. She'll have nothing but the baby to worry about. She'll be too busy with the baby, she won't have time for anything else. And then get her pregnant again," Elder William says.

"I don't think babies will do it. Not with her," Elder Steven says. The moonlight lights them up enough for me to see they're all worried. Worried about what I know.

"Kill her," Momma Edith says. Her voice is even, as if she doesn't care.

"We can't. We've made her an example so many times, everyone will ask questions," Elder Steven says.

"They can ask. We'll control the situation," Momma Edith says. "Like we always do."

"We also have to think of the sponsors," Elder William says.

All three nod their heads. *Sponsors?* What's a sponsor and why do they have to think of them?

"Then we can't kill her. But, if we can't control her, then…" Elder Steven says, and Momma Edith and Elder William both nod their heads again.

"I've got a meeting, and I need to be there by nine. If I don't get going now, I won't make it. Call an early curfew tomorrow. I'll be back around ten. Make sure they're all in bed," Elder William says to both Elder Steven and Momma Edith.

Nine?

Meeting?

Ten?

Sponsors?

What are all these things they're talking about?

"Full moon in four nights. You know what that means?" Elder Steven says.

"Yep, it means you better knock that bitch up, or we're in trouble," Momma Edith says.

Elder Steven and Elder William laugh.

Full moon means Elder Steven and I will... *yuck.* I swallow back the bile in my throat. It also means I need to find a way to get out of here, very soon.

Elder William walks toward the part of the wall that's missing. "I'll stop at the store on the way back. What do you want?"

"Bourbon," Elder Steven replies quickly. "Lots and lots of bourbon. And pick up some Viagra. I'm gonna need it. I think she's going to be a wild one in the sack." I have no idea what he means.

"Chocolate. I need chocolate," Momma Edith says.

"Got it. Alcohol and chocolate. Anything else?" Both Elder Steven and Momma Edith shake their heads. "I'm going back out in a couple of days, so I can get anything else we want then."

"I'm getting married again, you better not miss it," Elder Steven says to Elder William.

"Miss my opportunity to watch you screwing her. Not a chance in hell."

Momma Edith laughs, as does Elder Steven, when he adds, "You're a pervert."

"Don't you know it." Then Elder William leaves through the hole in the wall, and slowly the missing section slides back into place.

Elder Steven and Momma Edith both walk away, not looking over their shoulder at the sliding wall.

I lay back and look up to the moon again. I'm so confused. This is what I've learned. They use words I don't understand. But I know Elder William will be leaving through the hole in the wall again, before I'm due to wed Elder Steven. This may be my only opportunity to get out of here.

And I'm going to leave, the same way Elder William does.

Through the hole in the wall.

I just need to figure out, how it works.

CHAPTER TWENTY

"LUNA, YOU SEEM quiet," Elder Steven says as I pour his drink in the dining room. The other Elders laugh. I offer him a weak smile, and nod my head. "What's happening in that cute head of yours?"

"I don't have anything to say," I reply as I walk around to all the Elders, and offer them a drink. Some wave me away, some grunt as they eat, indicating they want a drink.

I have many questions. But I can't ask the Elders, or anyone else. I can't risk them knowing I heard what they were talking about.

"Steven, you'll be taking a new bride soon," Elder Tom says. Again, there's more laughter. Why they are laughing, I don't know. It's almost like they're all sharing a personal joke. Something they don't want me to know. Something they insist on taunting me with.

"I will. And she's a great girl too." Elder Steven

turns to look at me. "Prime for the picking. In her most fruitful state." I want to vomit on him. But I bite on the inside of my cheek, to make sure I don't.

"Make sure she's with child," another Elder says. I'm too repulsed to see who spoke. And, I don't care.

"She'll be a baby breeding machine. I think I can have her birth a few quite quickly."

I hate how they're talking about me like I'm not here. It makes me want to say something, but I have to be careful. *Very careful.*

"Are you ready for your vows, Luna?" Elder Joshua asks.

The fact I know what the vows entails, makes my stomach churn. "Of course," I reply, then go stand in my spot. I look to Ava who's helping in the dining room, and she smiles eagerly at me. If only she knew what I do.

"The full moon is fast approaching."

Ugh, why do they have to keep talking about this? Maybe, because there's more to it than just the vows. I'm quickly learning, when they're so forceful about something, like curfew, something else is happening.

It's like they are trying to divert our attention away from something else.

Maybe they're trying the same thing now. Talk about the vows and wedding, to try and make me *not* see something else. Is that what they're doing?

This makes me extra attentive to everything.

Elder William isn't here yet, maybe he's still asleep. Or maybe, there's more to him not being here.

"Am I too late for food?" he asks as he enters the dining room, as if he knew I was thinking about him. "Luna, food." He snaps his fingers and doesn't even look at me.

I feel my eye twitch.

He makes my blood heat with anger.

I hurry to take food over to him, all while watching to see how he reacts. He talks to the other Elders, and ignores me. I place his food on his plate, then step back, waiting for further instructions. Well, that's how it looks to him, what I'm doing is watching everything. Watching all the Elders, and memorizing what they're saying. The conversation is loud and chaotic, so I stand between Elder William and Elder Steven and try to focus in on them. I figure, they're the Elders I keep seeing together, maybe, they're the ones who hold all the power.

"Curfew before sunset," Elder William says in a low voice to Elder Steven.

"I'll call it after we eat."

Elder William nods, and doesn't say anything else. But he looks over his shoulder to see if either Ava or I are listening. I'm preparing to fill their glasses, so I appear busy. Ava is standing on the other side of the room, waiting to be called on. I hope Elder William doesn't know I was listening.

Because I think this may be my last chance to get out of here alive. I don't think I'll be able to go through the trees to get out again. I have a feeling they'll have fixed the hole I made under the wire. They can't risk me trying to get out the same way. They're too smart to not fix it. So, I'm going to walk out, the way Elder William leaves, through the hole in the wall. I'll wait until everyone is asleep, and I'll sneak out.

If the Elders catch me, I hope they kill me. I can't live buried in these lies anymore.

"Luna, there's a meeting. Come on," Bethany says.

I wipe my hands down the front of my pinafore, and walk out behind her. I walk to the back of where the girls are. Cain sees me, and lowers his head to the ground. I need to talk to him, to make sure he knows, I don't hate him for whipping me. He had to. He had no choice.

"As you all know, the full moon is nearly upon us," Elder William announces.

I let out a long sigh.

"Luna will be taken as Elder Steven's bride."

Not if I can help it.

"To prepare for the vow ceremony, a curfew before sunset will be strictly enforced."

I hear a collection of grumbles, coming from both the men and the girls. The Elders smile. From everything I've been able to gather, when there's curfew, something big is happening. And I think, the wall will have a hole in it, so I'm going to get out.

"A few more matters to address. For everyone, the trees are out of bounds. Our dear Abigail wandered to the trees, and was struck down with the disease the trees carry. Unfortunately, the disease claimed her life."

Some of the girls begin to cry. "Not Abigail..." Clara says as tears roll down her cheeks.

"Those trees are going to kill us all if we go near them," I hear Bethany whisper.

If only they knew the truth. The trees aren't what will kill us, the Elders are.

"I know you and Abigail weren't friends, but you were still sisters. Like all of us." Ava grabs onto my hand, and squeezes.

"Abigail was..." I stop talking, not wanting to say what I think. The fact is, Abigail, like the rest of us, had been conditioned to believe everything the Elders say. Elder Steven killed Abigail. She didn't die because of some diseased trees. That's what they're telling us, because that's what they want us to believe. "Abigail was beautiful," I finally say, noticing how Ava is waiting for me to finish my sentence. "She was sweet, and beautiful." And she was. But they created this riff between us, for some unknown reason. And Abigail, believed it.

Why wouldn't she? She had no reason not to. But I do. I've seen a tiny fragment of the outside, and I'm prepared to sacrifice myself to see more of it. Because I don't believe there's death and disease beyond the wall.

Elder William keeps talking, and I turn off to what he's saying. I don't want to hear any more lies or deceit coming from him or any of the Elders. I'm sick of them.

"Are you coming?" Ava asks, snapping me out of my heavy mindset.

"Of course." I smile.

"Luna, can we talk?" his voice calms me, and I don't need to turn around to know it's Cain. I don't need to see him, to know. I just know.

"I'll be in to help you when…" I pointedly tilt my head toward Cain.

Ava looks at me, then him, then back to me. Turning, I search for Elder Steven. If he sees us together, he's sure to punish me, or worse, Cain. "Please?" Cain pleads. The men don't need to plead, all they have to do is instruct, and as girls, we must obey.

I look at Cain's face, he's got black circles beneath his eyes, and he looks like he's not eating. "Of course." I look over my shoulder, making sure Ava has left. "But not here," I whisper.

Cain nods, and starts toward the wall. That's one place we can talk freely, where he's not a man, and I'm not a girl. Where we're equal. We get to the wall, and Cain sits on the grass. He crosses his legs, and drops his head into his hands. "I'm sorry, Luna. I didn't want to…"

"I know. You don't have to apologize." I sit beside him, too close. Close enough that I'm positive if the Elders see us, I'll be whipped. And I know Elder Steven will make Cain do it. Because Elder Steven is nasty, and cruel.

"I do, I have to say I'm so sorry. I haven't slept, I can barely eat. The guilt inside, it's destroying me."

"It wasn't you; it was Elder Steven. He made you do that to me." I reach out and grab his hand, prepared to face the consequences of touching someone other than Elder Steven. "Cain." I squeeze his hand. He lifts his chin, and I see exactly how much this is hurting him. He looks to our linked fingers and gives me the smallest of smiles. "It's not something you have to apologize for."

"But I hurt you."

"The part that hurt me most, was not the whipping, but the pain in your eyes as you were doing it. You had no choice." I hate to think what could've happened to him if he hadn't whipped me.

"I should've…"

"You couldn't," I answer the words he wants to say. "You couldn't say no. The Elders are the ones who protect us." I hate saying this to Cain. But I know, after I leave, they'll hurt Cain to see if he knows where I am. And I can't put him in danger. "They protect us from evil, Cain. They're our family. We need to trust in them."

Cain lets go of my hand, and pushes away from me. He stands and walks closer to the wall, putting distance between us. "What's happened to you, Luna?"

My heart beat spikes. What does he know? "What do you mean?" I stand, and close the distance between us.

"You've changed. Since you were ill and they had to isolate you, you've changed."

"I have?"

"How sick were you? Because since then, you've been really different. It's like, something changed inside of you."

Something did. The Elders aren't who they say they are. They beat me. They're cruel. "I don't know what you're talking about. I'm still me. I'm still Luna."

"No, something's different."

I have to change the conversation, or I might snap and tell him why I'm different and what I'm going to do at curfew. Stepping closer to him, I raise my hand and cup his face. He closes his eyes and lets out a deep sigh. I wish I could wrap my arms around his tall body to hold him. I just want to be close to him. But I know, that's too much. Touching him is putting us at risk. "Cain, I want you to remember something."

Taking my hand away, he opens his eyes instantly, as if he's missing my touch. I miss his. "What?" he asks.

"No matter what happens. I love you."

He smiles, then narrows his eyes. "What's going to happen, Luna? Are you sick? You told me you'd rather clean Elder Steven's bathroom then be near me. I don't understand. Now you're telling me you love me. What aren't you telling me?" he asks. Stepping forward, he places his hands on my shoulders, and I want to grab him and run.

"I'm not sick." I can feel my eyes tearing. "I just need you to know, I love you and I'll never stop loving you."

"Has this got to do with the vows you're about to take part in? I can try and talk to Elder Steven, tell him you're not ready. But you're so close to being of age, I don't know if I can stop it."

"No! Please, Cain, don't try to stop it! It has to happen. I just…" I pull away from him, and back up. "I need you to know, I wish we could be together." I point to myself, then to him. "Just know, whatever happens, I love you. I've always loved you."

Turning, I walk away, fast. I can't bear to look at him, and not tell him what I'm about to do.

But this way is safest.

I'll find a way to come back and get him out too. I have to.

CHAPTER TWENTY-ONE

"Luna?"

"Yes, Ava." I turn in bed, pretending to be tired. I know curfew has begun, and I also know this is definitely my last chance to get out, before I wed Elder Steven.

"Will you tell us about it?"

"About what?"

"About your vows with Elder Steven? I think we'd all like to know what happens." I hear a collective agreement from all the girls in the bedroom. "Once you're wed, you won't sleep with us again, you'll be in the rooms with his other wives. I can't believe, we'll have to call you Sister Luna once you wed."

"Please, I don't want to be called that."

"But we have to. It's how things are once you become an Elder's wife."

I don't want to think about what *can* happen.

All I want to think about, is everyone going to sleep, so I can sneak out. "I'm tired. And excited," I say, trying to muster the emotion through the tone in my voice. But, I'm dead inside. Until I can get out of here, I'll remain dead.

"Shhh," Bethany hushes us. "Luna needs her beauty sleep. When the sun rises, everything will be different."

I hope so.

There's some more talking, but all the girls quiet down fairly fast. Ava falls asleep first, her breathing evening out. Then all the girls follow, just like we always do. With the exception of me. I'm waiting until I know the darkness of the night will hide me. But the light from the moon will be enough to guide me out of here.

I'm nervous. Really nervous. I want to jump out of bed, and run to Cain, grab him by the hand and run away from here. But I can't. I can't get Cain away from here until I know what dangers lie beyond the wall, I can't risk him. He means too much to me.

Carefully listening to everything, my entire body is hyperaware of noises. I need to make sure I get out without being seen.

Before I know it, all the girls in the bedroom are asleep. I play this in my head over and over again. If I'm seen, I need to run, and keep running until they can't catch me. If I'm caught, I'll beg them to kill me. If they don't, I have to find a way to kill myself, because I can't keep living here. Not now I know what they're capable of and all the lies they keep telling us.

I slowly push the covers off my body, and wait to see if I wake Ava, or any other girl. They don't stir.

One of the girls coughs, and I freeze. But she goes back to sleep.

I slide my leg out of bed and feel for the floor. When my toes find the cold floor, I drop to it. My heart is going crazy. Like nothing I've ever felt before. My skin has a fine sheen of sweat covering it, and I can't seem to calm my rapid breathing.

Get it together, Luna.

Closing my eyes, I try and get an image of the outside. The brief encounter I had with what's beyond the wall is giving me enough determination to focus.

Opening my eyes, I reach for my shoes, pick them up, and head straight to the door. I put my ear to it, and can hear voices. They're muffled, but I can hear Elder Joshua, Elder Tom and I think Elder Steven. His voice is more distant and unclear.

Panic rises. I can't go out through the door. I stay listening, but I know, if I stay like this, somebody will catch me.

I have to make my move *now*.

Looking around, I do the only thing I can. I tiptoe over to the window, and squeeze between

Catherine's bed and the wall. She stirs and I freeze. Catherine has never really liked me, and I know she'll raise the dead with her screaming if she thinks I'm doing anything wrong.

But, Catherine turns in the bed to face Justine. Her breathing evens out again, and I continue trying to move toward the window as quietly as I can.

My rapid heartbeat keeps my mind focused. The knowledge of what's beyond the wall keeps me wanting to move toward it.

Reaching the window, I slide it up, little by little. Finally, when the window is open, I look around the room, making sure the girls are all still asleep. I listen, to ensure the Elders or Mommas aren't near.

I'm so close.

I can't get caught now. I just... *can't.*

Thankfully this window is large and low, so I slide my bottom on the edge, and look around again. I swing my leg out, straddling the window, then slide the other over and jump out.

I'm out.

This is it.

Ducking down, I keep listening for any possible movement.

The moon is nearly above, ducking in and out of the clouds, which means the light will make it easier for me to see, but it'll also make it easier for the Elders to see me. I have to go. And I have to go now.

Remaining as low as possible, I run toward the wall, where I've seen the hole. I stay hidden, concealed by dark patches of the few trees and the shadows of the houses.

When I get to where I've seen the hole, I lay flat on the ground, hoping the earth can conceal me if they discover I'm not in bed.

"Please," I whisper to myself. "Please, let the hole appear. Let me find my way out."

Closing my eyes, I beg for the hole to open.

I wait in the grass on the ground, and suddenly, it begins to rain. The drops are light at first, but when a huge clap of thunder sounds, the rain falls with tremendous force.

I'm not going back. I won't let the rain stop me.

The water falls heavier and heavier, until I can barely see or hear anything. I roll onto my stomach, and watch the wall, waiting for it to open.

If I can't see through the rain, that means, they won't be able to see through it either. Which means, they won't notice *me*, not until they find the bed empty at sunrise. This is the most perfect chance for me to leave my life from behind the wall.

As I'm watching, the most amazing thing happens. Part of the wall slides aside, and reveals the huge hole. I want to stand and run, but I know Elder William will be on his way to the hole. If he sees me, I won't get away. This is my only chance.

I wait.

And wait.

The rain gets heavier, eases, then gets heavier again. My clothes are soaked through to my skin. The rain is cold, and I shiver as I wait for Elder William to go through the hole first.

I can't be seen. I need to hold strong, and wait.

From the corner of my eye, I see him. Elder William. He runs toward the wall with something over his head. I know it's him by his body shape. He's tall and wiry, but he still has broad shoulders. He's not as tall as Elder Steven, nor as big as him. Elder Steven is much taller, and much thicker.

Elder William makes his way through the hole.

This is it. I won't get a chance like this again.

I look around, careful to make sure the Elders aren't near. None of them are out here. The rain must be keeping them in.

Standing, though still low to the ground, I run toward the hole.

I stay as close to the wall as I can, not be seen by Elder William, or anyone who may be watching. I peek out through the hole. Elder William gets into a little bus, a dark little bus. I wait.

This is happening too fast.

I should stay here. I shouldn't leave, I don't know what's out there.

Hesitating, I watch as the dark little bus leaves.

Getting smaller and smaller.

We are your family. Beyond the wall is death. Beyond the wall is evil. You will die if you leave. Only we can protect you.

Suddenly, the wall begins to slide back in place to close the hole. Slowly, the gap narrows.

We are your family. Beyond the wall is death. Beyond the wall is evil. You will die if you leave. Only we can protect you.

I don't know what to do. If I step through the wall, then I'm leaving Cain behind.

I can't leave him here, alone. I need to stay with Cain, protect him from them.

I take a step back, away from the wall.

The voice in my head keeps telling me how only they can protect me. I'm torn. I don't know what to do.

The wall is closing.

I'm confused.

I have to go, I can't stay.

Without thinking, I run toward the hole, slide through, and get out.

The hole is closing, and I hide against the wall. I did it.

I did it.

The wall makes a jarring movement as it closes, but surprisingly, it's not loud. Maybe the rain is muffling the sound.

"Have I made a mistake?" I scold myself. Even

if I have, there's no way back. I have to keep moving forward.

The little bus is now gone, and I don't know in which direction it's gone. It doesn't matter. I just need to make sure I don't get caught. And if I do, plead for them to kill me.

I can do this. *I can do this.*

I *will* do this.

There's no turning back.

CHAPTER TWENTY-TWO

THE RAIN HASN'T stopped. The moon is moving across the land, and soon the sun will replace it.

I'm walking without a clue as to where I'm going. I hope to find the people I've found before. I try to walk where the trees are, but there's nothing out here. No trees, nothing.

My mouth is parched, and my clothes are completely drenched through. My shoes make a squeaking sound as I walk along, and I wiggle my toes in the wet shoes. The back of my shoe is rubbing against my foot, and creating a blister. I can feel the pain as they continue to rub. I want to take my shoes off, but I don't know what else I may encounter. I can't risk hurting the bottom of my feet.

The sun rises, and hurts my eyes. My mouth is becoming drier, though my clothes are still wet. The rain is easing, only just. Opening my mouth, I try to get rainwater in so I can swallow. Anything has to be better than nothing. Bright colors cover the sky above me, and I try to walk toward the end of the beautiful colors.

My stomach rumbles.

I feel weak. Like I've walked for many sunrises and sunsets. Dragging my feet, I try to keep going.

Stumbling, I trip over something. I catch myself before I fall.

The sun is over the top of me again, the rain has now stopped, and I feel like every part of me is shutting down.

Ahead of me, I see a body of water, running toward it, it disappears before I get to it.

"What?" I ask myself as I collapse to the ground and try to drink from the water that's not here now. "Get up," I say to myself. "Keep moving."

My body is giving up on me, but I will myself to keep going.

We are your family. Beyond the wall is death. Beyond the wall is evil. You will die if you leave. Only we can protect you. No, no you're not. You will never protect me.

Luna, keep going, don't stop.

Dragging my lethargic body up, I keep walking. Slowly.

Everything hurts.

And I'm so thirsty. I need water. I need water now. I'm not sure if I'm going to survive if I don't get water soon. The sun is hot, but fading quickly.

It disappears, and darkness rapidly overtakes the day.

I don't know where I am. I don't know where I'm going.

Did I imagine those people? Is there really nothing out here? Is there death and illness?

We are your family. Beyond the wall is death. Beyond the wall is evil. You will die if you leave. Only we can protect you. The voice in my head keeps repeating as Elder Steven stands over me and beats me. I'm not sure I can keep going. I don't know where I am. There is nothing around me. Nothing. I should've stayed behind the wall. I shouldn't have left.

I should've stayed to wed Elder Steven. He's a nasty Elder, but…

No, no 'buts.' Keep going. You'll find something.

The moon is rising again, this time full and bright. Elder Steven would be telling me his vows, and Elder William would be standing in the room, watching us wed.

No, that can't be all I'm made for. To bear Elder Steven's young, to be nothing more than a girl. I have to be more. All the whippings, all the questions, everything I've seen and had happen to me, they have to be for a reason.

Elder William leaves by going through the hole in the wall, he must be going somewhere. But, where? I'm searching for the 'where.'

I don't know if I can do this. With hunger and thirst circling my already exhausted body, my steps slow. But I can't let them find me. If they do, they'll take me back to behind the wall.

We are your family. Beyond the wall is death. Beyond the wall is evil. You will die if you leave. Only we can protect you.

"No! No, you're not. You were never my family," I yell and try to hit the side of my head, hoping to dislodge the voice.

You can't do this.

"Yes, I can." I grab at my hair, and try to pull. The voice is of Elder Steven. His cruel eyes taunt me.

You won't survive without me.

"Get out of my head!" I scream at him again.

The moon is high above me, but I'm determined to keep going. I need to get somewhere. I need to find something that tells me this wasn't the wrong decision.

I hear something. "What's that?" I ask as I try to run toward the noise. It's close, but not close enough for me to see what's making the sound.

My throat is dry and sore, and my feet are dragging. But I need to get to where the noise is.

"Little busses," I say as I see so many of them going back and forth. I don't understand them. What are they doing?

I walk toward them. They're going fast, much faster than I can run. Even faster than Cain can run.

The moon is concealing me, but I need to see what these little busses are. What they're doing. There are so many. I don't understand.

I step closer to them.

Suddenly, my mouth isn't dry anymore. It's wet from all the saliva pooling in it. My eyes are wide open, and my pulse rapidly hammers inside my body. This is it. It's here I'll find the diseased and dead.

The tortured souls the Elders tell us about.

I make my way even closer.

Little busses zoom past so fast, the wind from their passing blows my hair up around my face.

I step even closer.

A little bus swerves around me, and someone yells something.

Another little bus does the same thing. "Get off the road you idiot," they scream. Road? Idiot? Frustration is building. They're saying words and I don't understand what they mean.

As I keep walking, more little buses zoom past me. All are swerving. What's happening? What are they doing? Do they think I'm one of the diseased? Are they trying to get away from the tortured? From death?

Bright lights shine in my face. A blue light, and a red light.

There's lots of noise. I don't know where it's

coming from. A little bus with the red and blue lights stops next to me.

I stand, watching the red and blue lights. It's mesmerizing. It goes around and around. But the noise hurts my ears. I put my hands over my ears, but can't seem to close my eyes. The lights are so pretty. So beautiful. I've never seen anything like them before. I want to touch them, but the noise is deafening and I don't dare uncover my ears. Suddenly, the noise stops.

"Are you okay?" A girl gets out of the little bus. She walks toward me, carefully.

I step back when she comes closer. She has strange eyes. "Are you sick?" I ask.

She looks over her shoulder, and I notice there's a man standing beside her. Is he an Elder? Is she a Momma? "What?" the girl asks.

"Are you sick?" I point to her eyes. "Your eyes are different. Is that from disease?"

"What?" the man asks.

I look at him, and notice how black he is. It frightens me. "Are you burned? Did you burn in a fire?" I step back, not sure what's wrong with them. I don't want to get sick. I cover my mouth with my hand so I don't get what they have.

They look at each other. Then back to me. "What's your name?" the man asks.

"Are you an Elder? Are you a Momma? You're wearing matching clothes." I point to their clothes and can't help but wonder why she's allowed to wear pants.

"What's your name?" the girl asks as she steps closer to me. But her eyes scare me. I don't want her disease. I don't want to get sick.

"Luna," I reply. "Are you sick?" I point again to her eyes and the man's black skin.

The girl looks over at the black man. She shakes her head at me. "I'm half-Chinese," she says.

"And I'm African-American," he replies.

"What's that?" I ask.

They look to each other with raised brows. Both turn and stare at me. "Where are you from, Luna?" the man asks, slowly.

"I'm calling this in. Something's wrong," the girl says. I don't understand what she's saying, but my skin raises goosebumps in response.

"Luna?" the girl says. I look to her. "What's your surname?"

I tilt my head. "My what?"

"Your last name. Your first name is Luna, and your last name is what?"

"My name is Luna." The man steps forward, and I step back. He notices my uneasiness around him. Can I catch the black off his skin? Can it rub off? "Did it hurt?"

"Did what hurt?" his voice is gentler.

"When you were burned. Did it hurt?"

"I've never been burned."

"But, your skin is all black. Is that not from

being in a fire?"

"Luna, where did you say you came from?" he asks again.

I point behind me. He looks over my shoulder. "From behind the wall," I say.

The girl with the funny eyes, and the black man stare at me, then each other.

"The wall?" the girl with the strange eyes asks.

I nod my head. "Yes, God's Haven." She's staring at me, like I've said something wrong. The man's mouth is open, and his eyes are narrow. They make him look like the girl with the funny eyes. Neither says anything. I nod and point again, before I repeat, "I came from behind the wall."

Luna is no longer caged behind the wall. But, what happens now she's out?

ALSO BY MARGARET MCHEYZER

Addiction

Drugs ruin people's lives.

I should know, they destroyed mine.

I'm Hannah and I got hooked on ice. What started as a trickle, ended with a tsunami washing everything away; my family, my life.

I'm not sure you're ready to read my story; it's real and confronting.

Open the book, read the pages and see how easy it is for anyone to get addicted.

Ice affects all types of people. It doesn't discriminate. It will SCREW. YOU. UP.

Drowning

I'm a cutter.

I cut because I find solace in it.

I cut because it helps calm my frantic mind.

I cut because the voice inside my head tells me to.

I cut because this is the only way I know how to handle life.

The Gift

I have something people want. I have something they cannot take or steal. I have something they'd kill for.

The something I have, isn't a possession, it's more.

Much, much more.

It's a gift.

It's part of me.

The Curse

It's been the butterfly effect.

I changed the course of my life because I warned a man.

I thought what I had was a gift, but it's quickly turning into my curse.

Now I realize I'm much more than a girl with an ability.

Because now... I'm becoming a weapon.

Dying Wish

I have three major loves in my life: my family, my best friend Becky, and ballet. Elijah Turner is quickly becoming the fourth.

He's been around as long as I can remember. But now he's much more than just the annoying guy at school.

My life was working out perfectly...until it got turned upside down.

Mistrust

I'm the popular girl at school.

The one everyone wants to be friends with.

I have the best boyfriend in the world, who's on the basketball team.

My parents adore me, and I absolutely love them. My sister and I have a great relationship too.

I'm a cheerleader, I have a high GPA and I'm liked even by the teachers.

It was a night which promised to be filled with love and fun until…something happened which changed everything.

Ugly

This is a dark YA/NA standalone, full-length novel. Contains violence and some explicit language

If I were dead, I wouldn't be able to see.

If I were dead, I wouldn't be able to feel.

If I were dead, he'd never raise his hand to me again.

If I were dead, his words wouldn't cut as deep as they do.

If I were dead, I'd be beautiful and I wouldn't be so...ugly.

I'm not dead...but I wish I was.

Chef Pierre

Holly Walker had everything she'd ever dreamed about – a happy marriage and being mum to beautiful brown-eyed Emma - until an accident nineteen months ago tore her world apart. Now she's a widow and single mother to a boisterous little 7-year-old girl, looking for a new start. Ready to take the next step, Holly has found herself a job as a maître d' at Table One, a once-acclaimed restaurant in the heart of Sydney. But one extremely arrogant Frenchman isn't going to be easy to work with...

Twenty years ago, Pierre LeRoux came to Australia, following the stunning Aussie girl he'd fallen in love with and married. He and his wife put their personal lives on hold, determined for Pierre to take Sydney's culinary society by storm. Just as his bright star was on the upswing, tragedy claimed the woman he was hopelessly in love with. He had been known as a Master Chef, but since his wife's death he has become known as a monster chef.

Can two broken people rebuild their lives and find happiness once more?

Smoke and Mirrors

Words can trick us.

Smoke obscures objects on the edge of our vision.

A mirror may reflect, but the eye sees what it wants.

A delicate scent can evoke another time and place, a memory from the past.

And a sentence can deceive you, even as you read it.

Grit

Recommended for 18 years and over

Alpha MC Prez Jaeger Dalton wants the land that was promised to him.

Sassy Phoenix Ward isn't about to let anyone take Freedom Run away from her.

He'll protect what's his.

She'll protect what's hers.

Jaeger is an arrogant ass, but he wants nothing more than Phoenix.

Phoenix is stubborn and headstrong, and she wants Jaeger out of her life.

Her father lost the family farm to gambling debts, but Jaeger isn't the only one who has a claim to the property.

Sometimes it's best to let things go.

But sometimes it's better to fight until the very end.

Yes, Master

**** This prologue contains distressing content. It is only suited for readers over 18. ****

Also contains M/M, M/M/F, M/F and F/F scenes.

My uncle abused me.

I was 10 years old when it started.

At 13 he told me I was no longer wanted because I had started to develop.

At 16 I was ready to kill him.

Today, I'm broken.

Today, I only breathe to survive.

My name's Sergeant Major Ryan Jenkins and today, I'm ready to tell you my story.

A Life Less Broken
*****CONTAINS DISTRESSING CONTENT. 18+*****

On a day like any other, Allyn Sommers went off to work, not knowing that her life was about to be irrevocably and horrifically altered.

Three years later, Allyn is still a prisoner in her own home, held captive by harrowing fear. Broken and damaged, Allyn seeks help from someone that fate put in her path.

Dr. Dominic Shriver is a psychiatrist who's drawn to difficult cases. He must push past his own personal battles to help Allyn fight her monsters and nightmares.

Is Dr. Shriver the answer to her healing?

Can Allyn overcome being broken?

My Life for Yours

He's lived a life of high society and privilege; he chose to follow in his father's footsteps and become a Senator.

She's lived a life surrounded with underworld activity; she had no choice but to follow in her father's footsteps and take on the role of Mob Boss.

He wants to stamp out organized crime and can't be

bought off.

She's the ruthless and tough Mob Boss where in her world all lines are blurred.

Their lives are completely different, two walks of life on the opposite ends of the law.

Being together doesn't make sense.

But being apart isn't an option

HiT Series Box Set

HiT 149

Anna Brookes is not your typical teenager. Her walls are not adorned with posters of boy bands or movie stars. Instead posters from Glock, Ruger, and Smith & Wesson grace her bedroom. Anna's mother abandoned her at birth, and her father, St. Cloud Police Chief Henry Brookes, taught her how to shoot and coached her to excellence. On Anna's fifteenth birthday, unwelcome guests join the celebration, and Anna's world is never the same. You'll meet the world's top assassin, 15, and follow her as she discovers the one hit she's not sure she can complete – Ben Pearson, the current St. Cloud Police Chief and a man with whom Anna has explosive sexual chemistry. Enter a world of intrigue, power, and treachery as Anna takes on old and new enemies, while falling in love with the one man with whom she can't have a relationship.

Anna Brookes in Training

Find out what happened to transform the fifteen-year-old Anna Brookes, the Girl with the Golden Aim, into the deadly assassin 15. After her father is killed and her home destroyed, orphan Anna Brookes finds herself homeless in Gulf Breeze, Florida. After she saves Lukas from a deadly attack, he takes her in and begins to train her in the assassin's craft. Learn how Lukas's unconventional training hones Anna's innate skills until she is as deadly as her mentor.

HiT for Freedom

Anna has decided to break off her steamy affair with Ben Pearson and leave St. Cloud, when she suspects a new threat to him. Katsu Vang is rich, powerful, and very interested in Anna. He's also evil to his core. Join Anna as she plays a dangerous game, getting closer to Katsu to discover his real purpose, while trying to keep Ben safe. Secrets are exposed and the future Anna hoped for is snatched from her grasp. Will Ben be able to save her?

HiT to Live

In the conclusion to the Anna Brookes saga, Ben and his sister Emily, with the help of Agent rescue Anna. For Anna and Ben, it's time to settle scores…and a time for the truth between them. From Sydney to the Philippines and back to the States, they take care of business. But a helpful stranger enters Anna's life, revealing more secrets…and a plan that Anna wants no part of. Can Anna and Ben shed their old lives and start a new one together, or will Anna's new-found family ruin their chances at a happily-ever-after?

Binary Law (co-authored)

Ellie Andrews has been receiving tutoring from Blake McCarthy for three years to help her improve her grades so she can get into one of the top universities to study law. And she's had a huge crush on him since she can remember.

Blake McCarthy is the geek at school that's had a crush on Ellie since the day he met her.

In their final tutoring session, Blake and Ellie finally become brave enough to take the leap of faith.

But, life has other plans and rips them apart. Six years later Blake and his best friends Ben and Billy have built a successful internet platform company 3BCubed, while Ellie is a successful and hardworking lawyer specializing in Corporate Law.

3BCubed is being threatened with a devastatingly large plagiarism case and when it lands on their lawyers desk, it's handed to the new Corporate Lawyer to handle and win.

Coincidence or perhaps fate will see Blake and Ellie pushed back together.

Binary Law will have Blake and Ellie propelled into a life that's a whirl wind of catastrophic events and situations where every emotion will be touched. Hurt will be experienced, happiness will be presented and love will be evident. But is that enough for Blake and Ellie be able to live out their own happily ever after?